Gilles Pétel was born and raised in Dunkirk. After studying philosophy at the Université de Nice, he spent several years abroad teaching. His first novel *Le Métier dans le sang* was published in 1996.

Emily Boyce is in-house translator at Gallic Books. She lives in London.

Jane Aitken studied history at St Anne's College, Oxford. She is a publisher and translator from the French.

Under the Channel

Under the Channel

Gilles Pétel

Translated from the French
by Emily Boyce and Jane Aitken

Gallic Books
London

A Gallic Book

First published in France as *Sous la Manche* by Éditions Stock 2012

Copyright © Éditions Stock 2012

English translation copyright © Gallic Books 2014

First published in Great Britain in 2014 by Gallic Books, 59 Ebury Street,
London, SW1W 0NZ

A CIP record for this book is available from the British Library

ISBN 978-1-908313-66-9

Typeset in Fournier MT by Gallic Books

Printed in the UK by CPI (CR0 4YY)

2 4 6 8 10 9 7 5 3 1

In memory of my mother

For Balthazar

*To Guy, for his invaluable information on
the French judiciary police*

Identity is the very devil
Wittgenstein

1

Perhaps it was enough just to have made it to St Pancras despite the Friday traffic, to have noted the time of the train on the departures board and to have savoured the prospect of the journey, the arrival at Gare du Nord, the glass of champagne at Terminus Brasserie. Was it really worth actually making the trip?

John glanced briefly at his watch, a Rolex he had bought five years earlier. Five years already? he wondered. It was five o'clock now. His train left at 18.05, so he would definitely have time for a couple of pints of Guinness at the Black Swan, a pub he was getting to know quite well.

John Burny was treating himself to a weekend in Paris, as he often did. Two nights in a hotel, a few good meals and some action would recharge his batteries. He would be back at work on Monday morning revitalised.

To John, the weekend started the moment he closed the smart, wide glass door of the Chelsea estate agent where he worked. The anticipation of the journey that lay ahead made him see everything in a different light. He was already somewhere else without having taken a single step. The run-of-the-mill corner pub he often stopped at after work suddenly had a renewed appeal, and he started to regret not being able to drink there this weekend. He felt ready for new experiences and was falling in love again with the proud city he had been so in awe of when he arrived as a young man. He had come to London barely twenty years old from his native Glasgow. His accent betrayed not only his country of origin but also his modest background. He quickly learned how to turn this to his advantage. The rich clients he served at the agency found him entertaining and were charmed as much by the good-looking man's broad Scots vowels as by the luxurious apartments he showed them. They liked John for his lack of pretension which they judged came from him being a provincial with a strong accent. Now that his time was entirely his own, with a train ticket in hand and three-quarters of an hour to spare, John looked at London with a new desire to make the most of it and to conquer it.

'Shit,' he realised. 'It's raining.'

Hurrying across the Euston Road by St Pancras, John was almost run over by a double-decker. The bus driver blasted his horn, forcing John to make for the pavement in two giant strides, which almost catapulted him into the arms of an Indian man waiting to cross. Embarrassed,

John mumbled his apologies, before noticing how attractive the young man was. He was about to speak to him, but the man had already taken off. John watched him admiringly as he crossed, moving gracefully in his white tunic. Then he vanished, swallowed up by the mouth of the tube. The one good thing about the Empire, thought John, was that it had brought variety to the drabness of old England. The weather didn't look like brightening up. A north-easterly wind had begun to blow and the cloud was thickening. The rain was setting in. He was now desperate for a pint.

'Guinness,' he yelled to get the attention of the barman, probably a Brazilian judging from his accent and facial features. He wore a look of constant surprise and, in common with many of Rio's *Cariocas*, was perma-tanned.

He was a good-looking guy, doing the best job he could – quite a bad job – of keeping up with the orders being thrown at him from all sides of the bar. The young Englishwoman beside him was making heavy work of drying a glass, ignoring the baying hordes and staring up at the wall-mounted flatscreen TV, which was tuned to a news channel broadcasting stories on a loop. Since the beginning of that week, all anyone had talked about was the collapse of Lehman Brothers. The picture showed trainee bankers trailing out onto the street with a pocket summary of their careers – a computer, three or four folders and a handful of plastic wallets –

shoved hastily inside cardboard boxes of the kind used for supermarket deliveries. Repeated over and over like the images of 9/11, the footage made a deep impression on viewers who were always receptive to a catastrophe, whether ecological, terrorist or, indeed, financial. In spite of himself, John turned to look at the ill-boding screen, as fascinated as everyone else by the strings of negative numbers flashing up in a box to one side of the picture. It was possible to take in the fluctuations of the stock market and the looks of despair on the faces of the Lehman Brothers staff all at once. John knew the figures. His boss, a wily old Scot, had called his two agents to a meeting that very morning in order to discuss the state of the market. House prices in London were falling; sales were slowing down. The picture onscreen had abruptly changed and now depicted the aftermath of a car bombing in Baghdad. Seventy-two people had been killed. At the sight of the victims' maimed bodies, a section of the audience had to avert their eyes. John realised his glass was empty.

'Guinness,' he yelled again.

Was it really such a great idea to splash three thousand pounds on a trip to Paris? John paused to consider. 'If I'm going to get sacked next week,' he thought to himself, 'I may as well blow the bank one last time – while the banks are still open.' When he got back, he would tighten his belt. His pint had just been set down on the bar in front of him. The sight of it lifted his spirits. The financial crisis was just a blip. The *Financial Times* was predicting the economy would bounce back in January. Worst-case scenario, February or March. The company would get through it. The venerable Mr McGallan wouldn't give up his pride and joy that easily. John slowly wet his lips with the cool, white, thick head of his Guinness. How could his boss even consider getting rid of him? There was no way Kate could cope alone. But would that always be the case?

John sipped his second beer, his mind divided between background anxiety and the pleasure of the moment. This was a much more enjoyable pint than the first, which he had drunk too quickly, almost in one go. The same went for sex, it occurred to John. It was always better the second time; once the nervous fumbling was out of the way, it was more intense, more confident, more assured.

The previous weekend as he was leaving a performance of Mahler's last symphony at the Royal Albert Hall, John had met a young Saudi guy. The man had been innocently walking down Kensington Gore when John practically knocked him over in his hurry to flag down a taxi amid the crowds spilling out of the concert hall. The stunned look on the Saudi's face quickly gave way to one of pleasant surprise. John stopped in his tracks, gave up on the cab and struck up a conversation. The rest of the night had gone like a dream. Bar, club, hotel room at the Hilton where the guy had booked in for just over three weeks. They had seen each other again that Tuesday. They had made another date for this weekend. But — and this was a source of regret to him — if John was fond of second times, and the satisfaction of possessing what he had lusted after, the same could not be said of the third. It was one time too many. It made him feel trapped.

When preparing to leave the office, John had weighed up his options — Paris or Ali the Saudi — as if there was ever really any question in his mind. Just then, his colleague Kate had come over and asked him to get her a box of fruit jellies from Hédiard. She was mad about those sweets, and though she could easily get hold of them at Harrods or Fortnum's, she preferred to wait until a friend, such as John, could bring some back from France for her.

'Just a little box!' she added as her colleague's face dropped.

He didn't like being sent on shopping missions. Kate was taking advantage. On the other hand, John knew he could count on her to cover for him if he ever needed to slip out of the office. He could hardly turn down her modest request. The die was cast. Paris it was.

Outside the office, he had taken out his mobile phone and sent a message to the Saudi guy: 'Come down with beast of a cold. Staying in bed all weekend. Sorry.' A few seconds later he wrote him a second text: 'See you soon baby.'

17.25. Time was ticking on. John still hadn't quite made up his mind. The barman really wasn't half bad. He was currently serving a group of what could only be office workers, judging by their drab suits, blue and white checked shirts and ties in clashing colours that had been loosened on the way to the pub. The five friends huddled around the bar, talking loudly about football and women. They were, what, thirty? Thirty-five? And three of them already had receding hairlines and greying temples. Little pot bellies peeked through their checked shirts, a reminder of the fifteen pints they drank every weekend. Although John was forty-five, he was fairly sure he looked younger than every one of them. He ran his hand over his stomach to confirm this. It was almost washboard flat. Glancing back at the group, whose raucous laughter was attracting stares, he told himself it would nevertheless be a good idea to go to the gym five times a week rather than his usual three. He had to be careful not to let himself go, as so many others had. Not the barman, though, whom John could watch filling glasses at his leisure. It wasn't just his pretty face, with those exotic, rugged features. On top of that, he had incredible muscles, probably thanks to daily workouts. His biceps were especially impressive. Perfection. Good enough to eat. John was practically drooling when the barman turned round and shot him a huge smile. Taken aback, John felt a surge of heat through his body as his engine stirred into action. 'Son of a bitch!' he muttered to himself. By the time he had regained his composure and smiled back, the barman had returned to serving his customers in an outrageously friendly manner.

17.35. He should have left by now. With his first class ticket, John was allowed to check in up to ten minutes before the train's departure time, rather than the half-hour required of standard class passengers. Even so, the station would be busy on a Friday night, and there was bound to be a queue to get through security. If they were checking people thoroughly, as they increasingly did, John might be pushed back and risk missing his train. But wasn't that exactly what he wanted? He looked around for the barman and saw him busily serving at the other end of the bar. Meanwhile his colleague had finally got her arse in gear and was taking an order.

'What an airhead!' John said to himself. 'And as for the other one! Why run off when he's just been making eyes at me?'

He thought about moving to the other end of the bar to order a third pint and force that hunk to look at him again. What was he going to do in Paris? The need for this trip was becoming less and less clear to him. The weather would be just the same over there. Rain, for certain. France was going downhill. The food was often sub-standard and the service unfriendly. John was on the verge of calling the whole thing off. He glanced up to feast his eyes once more on the Brazilian, but he had disappeared, vanished, been abducted! Ridiculous as it was, a rush of panic swept over John, a sense of having been abandoned not only by the barman but by everyone in this old man's pub in which he was suddenly aware of being out of place in his smart polo shirt, designer jeans and luxury travel bag. London itself seemed like a distant, foreign city. He had not been born here. So why not go to Paris? In one decisive swoop John picked up his bag, turned his back on the bar and made his way out of the crowded pub as though charging across a battlefield. He must emerge victorious.

At the check-in barrier, the Afro-Caribbean girl on duty refused to let him through. He was too late. The train was leaving in less than ten minutes. The queue for the next one was already forming. John made his case: a client had held him up at work and then the Tube had delayed him further. He was expected in Paris. He simply had to take this train. The check-in assistant held an impeccably polite smile as John reeled off his excuses, but refused to budge. The minutes were ticking by. John was beginning to lose his cool. He asked to speak to the manager. The girl went on smiling but had ceased to listen. Other passengers were thronging around her asking for information, describing passport problems, an issue regarding their children. Can my daughter travel alone? Eventually the departure of the 18.05 was announced over the Tannoy.

'There, you see,' the girl said turning back to John,

whose face had drained of all colour. 'You couldn't have made it,' she added with a sneer of satisfaction. 'There's just enough time to exchange your ticket for the next train.'

John always travelled first class and bought a fully flexible ticket. He preferred to pay top whack and have the freedom to amend or cancel the booking if he changed his mind at the last minute. The same question was tapping away at him again. Why go? It seemed as though the whole universe was conspiring to keep him in London. It didn't usually take much to convince him to put off a trip. A glimpse of a good-looking face and the prospect of a bit of fun were enough to keep him out on the town all weekend, undoing in a flash his carefully laid plans. Why press on this time when everything was stacking up against him?

The only reason John could see for his own persistence was the date that lay ahead of him in Paris. For the past two weeks he had been exchanging steamy emails with a young Moroccan guy, whose photos had got him hot under the collar. Mohamed or Mustapha, John couldn't remember, was an apprentice butcher in the twentieth arrondissement. One of the pictures showed him posing proudly outside his shop in his apron and white hat. The two men had agreed to meet on the night of John's arrival, around eleven o'clock on Place de la Bastille. But Mohamed or Mustapha might very well stand him up and the whole thing would be a waste of time – and not for the first time. Already waiting in line for the next departure, John continued to weigh up the pros and cons. On the one hand there was Mustapha, who wasn't yet in the bag, and on the other was Ali, whom he knew too well. Wasn't it about time he broadened his horizons? Brazilian guys were gorgeous and they were ten a penny in London. The barman at the Black Swan could be a good place to start. John had reached this point in his deliberations when he found himself at the front of the queue. Without further thought, he asked for a ticket for the next departure.

'The 19.03?' the man behind the desk asked in a tone simultaneously obsequious and self-important, the tone the little people take on the rare occasion they find themselves in a position of power.

'Yes. A first class seat. I'm exchanging my ticket.'

'That train's full, sir.'

'What do you mean, *full*? It can't be!'

'It's full, sir,' the man repeated. He seemed to take pleasure in observing his customer's incredulous reaction.

Once again, as with the woman on the check-in desk, John attempted the impossible. His doubts had dissolved. He wanted to go to Paris and he *had to* take this train.

'Add another carriage!'

The man in front of him, a wizened old Indian fellow whose retirement was surely long overdue, would not be moved. John had to face facts. He would not be getting on this train. Paris now seemed to him like the most marvellous city in the world. Mohamed would be there waiting for him. An unforgettable night lay in store. Soon John would be stroking his date's hand, subtly, so no one else would see. Mustapha would shoot him a glance that sent thrills down his spine. They would walk the streets of Paris before diving into some hidden doorway for a kiss.

'Have you made up your mind, sir?'

'I'll take a seat on the last train.'

The last train left at 20.04. John quickly worked out he had ninety minutes before he needed to be back at the gate. It was too much time to sit around doing nothing, but not enough to attempt to do anything. There was no way he could contemplate leaving the area. By the time he got down to Soho to see if anyone was around, the train would have left without him. On the other hand, spending in excess of an hour traipsing around the station was a dismal prospect. 'I'd look like I was trying to pick someone up,' he thought wearily.

Out of habit, he glanced at his phone. He had no messages, obviously. His friends thought he had already left the country. He felt a twinge of sadness. How many friends could he really count on, when all was said and done? Six or seven, at most. Feeling increasingly sorry for himself, he realised it was more like five. Included in this revised total was the famous Ali of London, but John couldn't exactly claim Ali as a friend. Could he even refer to him as an acquaintance? So the number was four, in fact. Kate, David, Philip and Enrico, an Italian John had met some ten years earlier. They had carried on seeing one another fairly regularly, two or three times a year. Did that make him a friend? John held the phone up to his face again as though expecting it to perform a miracle. There was nothing lighting up the screen of the exorbitantly priced device. Three friends then, at the final count.

He had to snap out of this mood. John slid the phone inside one of the external pockets of his travel bag to try to put it out of his mind. Every cloud had a silver lining, however small that cloud had been to begin with. John's loneliness made him appreciate his freedom. He had taken the decision to get away for the weekend. He wanted to travel. Travel meant adventure, even if all he was embarking on was an apparently straightforward return trip to Paris. He had had to overcome one obstacle after another since leaving the office, after all. He pictured those climbers making their way up Everest, battling the cold, snow and avalanches. In his own small way, John told himself he had just faced a kind of avalanche. He had got out alive and that was the most important thing. All these thoughts of peaks and summits gave John the sudden urge to take the escalator to the upper level, from where you could watch the trains coming in and out. He was beginning to feel himself again. The great glass roof of St Pancras dazzled him, like the sun going down behind the slopes of Mont Blanc. The sky-blue canopy gave off a sense of majestic vastness. The enormous arch stood as a symbol of the power of the Empire.

'Fuck!' John said to himself. 'That's really something!'

It was the first time he had ever stopped to take a proper look at the station. He had passed through it so many times, but in his rush to catch a train or get home he had never even lifted his head to see where he was. Up ahead, the Brussels train was moving off. Once more seized with anxiety, John wondered if he wouldn't have been better off going to Belgium. He could be halfway there by now, comfortably ensconced in his first class single seat. But what would he have done with himself in Brussels? There was no one waiting for him there. Dark thoughts circled in his mind. He stared up at the roof. It was glorious, obviously. But now what? He hurried back down the escalator to the main concourse where he joined the ranks of commuters window-shopping at the smart boutiques while they waited for their trains. John's instincts told him to get out of the station. He needed air.

The rain was still falling and the wind had brought a chill to the air. Autumn had come early. A car raced by, ploughing through the wide puddle of oily water which had formed along the gutter and which John, standing on the edge of the pavement lost in thought, had failed to notice. He was soaked.

'Shit!' he shouted, turning back and heading inside the station. His mood having dipped once again, he told himself the old building must be worth investigating in greater depth. Bricks and mortar were his trade, after all. The lack of interest he had hitherto shown in the place put him to shame. But where should he start? He already knew the main concourse and the upper level. He decided to concentrate on the passages running off to the sides. John had years of experience showing buyers around lavish apartments, employing every sales trick in the book, effortlessly extolling the panoramic views, the dream living space worthy of the wealthiest clients, the rococo bedrooms, the cavernous entrance halls and all the unnecessary add-ons of a luxury abode. He loved describing places, using grandiose words to exalt what he always referred to as 'high-end specifications'; but now, before this display of neo-Gothic architecture, supposedly the very definition of wow-factor, he found himself at a loss. He wandered in and out of the various passageways, but nothing captured his attention and he kept a hurried pace. He found it all tiring to look at. He came back out onto the street five minutes later, overwhelmed. There was nothing to see in there. If tasked with selling St Pancras to a Punjabi nabob, on the other hand, John would no doubt have found the words to sing its praises. A stunning, must-see gem, perhaps.

Come to think of it, John never really looked at the apartments he showed people round. A true salesman, he made do with a quick scan around the rooms to get a feel for space, proportions, views. He would note down two or three key points about the style of the property – Victorian, Georgian or whatever – and that was it. This thought reminded him of something else. John had failed to secure an important sale the previous week. The potential buyer, a businessman from Muscat, had judged the price too high. The flat, a nicely presented two-bed, was on the market for two million pounds, and its owner, Mrs Dodd, would not listen to John's arguments. The market was heading downwards; there was even talk of a crash. Experts were predicting that prices might plummet thirty per cent in a matter of weeks, and the flat had already been on the market for four months. Mrs Dodd was an old rich widow who had inherited the property from her late husband, George Dodd, a distant descendant of a family of plantation owners in the West Indies.

'If I reduce the price,' she told John, 'I'll feel I'm being disloyal to George.' Besides, these oil barons from the Gulf were extremely rich. If they wanted to come over here and buy a home in London, they could jolly well pay for it, she added, sounding a note of peculiarly British pride. John watched his commission go up in smoke.

John's rumbling stomach called time on his

ruminations. Hunger gave him the excuse he had been waiting for to leave St Pancras again. Outside, there was no improvement in the weather. It was now chucking it down. On the other side of the road, two fast food outlets stood side by side, both offering cheap burgers and fried chicken. The smell of stale fat reached him fifty yards away. As he got closer, the stench made him gag. Looking through the windows, he saw scruffy diners at Formica tables, the strip lighting casting an unhealthy pallor over their faces. John hurried past, back to the Black Swan.

18.40. Peak time at the bar. Drinkers were spilling out onto the pavement. Huddling under their umbrellas, they leaned against the wall, gulping down their pints. After a brief moment of doubt, John sharpened his elbows and worked a path to the door. That's when the real problems started. A group of merry youths were leaving the pub, pushing John back out onto the cobbled street as they did so. There was nothing he could do: there were six or seven of them and only one of him. But before he had time to get worked up about it, he found himself being swept back the other way by another group, landing him back where he started on the doorstep. The bar, just yards from the entrance, seemed impossible to reach.

'I give up,' John said to himself, just as he collided with another group and ended up back on the pavement once more. Carrying his travel bag in one hand and umbrella in the other, he felt his strength diminishing. He was hungry and thirsty. The memory of the Brazilian barman bucked him up. Without further ado and almost without looking where he was going, John pushed open the swing doors, walked in and veered first right and then left, muttering his excuses, finally getting somewhere. But just as he laid his hand on the bar, a drunk came falling into him. Sporting an Arsenal shirt, the guy must have been at least six foot six, and John wobbled under the weight of him. As he tried to step back, the bloke slid to the floor and spewed the contents of his stomach – at least a dozen pints, by anyone's guess – at John's feet. A circle formed around them. The barman had already armed himself with a bucket and mop. A rancid toilet smell hit John's airways. The giant was pissing himself. The barman let out a groan of disgust. The circle of bystanders stood back a good yard.

'This can't be happening,' thought John, as a fellow drinker called over to ask if he and the giant were together. The question left him briefly speechless. 'Of course not!' he eventually replied, horrified at the idea he could be mistaken for having such poor taste. 'Am I really that much of a mess?' he asked himself, glancing down at his rain-soaked trousers. He had to get out of there, and fast. John now realised that the barman mopping the floor was not the one he had been hoping to see. The Brazilian must have finished his shift. A

Pole, judging by the accent, had replaced him. A good-looking blond, yes, but now was really not the time. On his way out of the pub, John passed two paramedics carrying a stretcher. They had come quickly.

John hurried across the main road. The stench of that man clung to his skin. He took a deep breath. The rain was coming down by the bucketload. What if the giant was dead? He might have wet himself on his way out, the muscles relaxing at the point of death. John felt a knot of anxiety forming inside his stomach. Was he too about to piss? He felt a sudden, urgent need to empty his bladder.

'Well that's just great,' he thought. 'I've had it.'

The two pints of Guinness he had knocked back an hour earlier were now making their presence felt.

'Shit!' he muttered, racing into the station in search of toilets. The flow of commuters was starting to dry up. John strode along the concourse looking left, right and straight ahead, to no avail. In his rush to locate the lavatories, he almost floored a Frenchman who had just got off the incoming train. Struggling with a map, he hadn't seen the Scotsman flying towards him at the speed of a fighter pilot. The Frenchman apologised, as though his mere presence on foreign soil was a reason to feel guilty. But John was already a dozen yards further on, still turning his head one way and the other.

'I've had it,' he told himself once more. He felt like he might keel over any second. 'Right. OK. I'll go through security and passport control and then I'm heading straight to the urinals.'

The woman with the permanent smile recognised him immediately. It was seven o'clock. John had actually turned up in good time for this train. Her smile broadened. John was among the first passengers to arrive. The woman was on her own with little to do. She would have liked to strike up a conversation but John didn't let her get a word in. He was already feeding his ticket into the mouth of the machine, which spat it out again as the barrier lifted. There was still security to get through. John threw his bag onto the conveyor belt without waiting to be asked. He set down his umbrella and took off his watch, shoes and belt, deaf to the words of the security officer who was telling him he really didn't need to bother with his shoes. John carried on regardless, now rooting through his pockets in search of stray coins, keys, any metal object likely to set off the detector and delay his progress. He would be forced to explain himself, to unzip his bag and open it wide, when all he could think about was one thing: 'If I don't piss, I've had it.' At passport control, he offered up his best Scottish smile along with his documents. Go ahead! A moment later, leaning against the wall of the urinals, he thought he had achieved nirvana. His face was the very picture of happiness. 'I'm alive!' The missed train, the rain, the giant, had all been forgotten.

*

The train doors closed automatically with a dull thud. The noise came as a relief, like a burst of oxygen coming to the aid of a deep-sea diver or a climber at the top of Everest struggling for air. John didn't know what to think about, but at least he could feel his muscles relaxing. 'Everything's good. Cool. I'm off.' The train was on time. Having taken his place in first class, John stretched out his legs and shamelessly sprawled in the comfort of his seat as the train started moving. Why go? He knew the answer now. Getting away gave you the feeling of starting over. Even if just for a couple of days, it was a clean slate each time. 'Goodbye Kate, goodbye Ali the Incredible, goodbye everyone, I'm off, I'm leaving, who knows when I'll be back again.' Just getting away for the weekend gave you the space to dream and to forget everyday life for a little while. The ball of anxiety lodged in John's stomach gradually ebbed away with each mile the train travelled. Soon there would be nothing left of it but an empty shell. John was on his way to Paris.

Row upon row of two-up-two-downs ran in front of John's absent gaze. Now and then, a warehouse or factory building broke up the monotony of the suburban landscape. Then suddenly they were in the countryside. Like disjointed images in a dream, the working-class homes had given way abruptly to a sleepy expanse of green as night fell over Kent. Fields floated in the twilight, languid with rain. The land was falling asleep, rocked by the slow and steady movement of the water. Lovely. Not far off the beauty of a Turner. John rubbed his eyes. He was almost asleep himself. When he next looked out of the window, it was dark. 8.30 p.m. The train would soon be entering the Channel Tunnel. The darkness over the farmland would be succeeded by that of the long tunnel. There wasn't much to tell between them. For a second, John caught sight of two little white lights flickering in the gloom. A moment later they were gone. Under the Channel there would be nothing to light the sky. Down at the bottom it was as dark as the grave, mused John, seized by the melancholy that sometimes hits once you have set off and there's no going back. The image of the drunken giant falling at his feet came back to him. A loud burst of laughter from an English couple sitting a few rows ahead shook him from his thoughts. They were quaffing a bottle of champagne. Judging by the tone of their voices, the man was in his fifties, she perhaps a little younger. They seemed intent on spending the entire journey drinking. And really, it occurred to John, what else was there to do to pass the time? A quarter of an hour later he was back in his seat armed with enough provisions to see him to the end of the longest tunnel: a bottle of champagne, a bag of peanuts, a ham sandwich and two beers, just in case the train broke down.

Lo and behold, the train had begun to slow its pace.

Outside, floodlights rained down on a futuristic expanse of steel and concrete. Barbed wire fences ran alongside the rails. The train was approaching the entrance of the tunnel. The blinding lights went out in the flick of a switch.

'We're in,' thought John, tearing his gaze from the window. The gaping mouth of the tunnel had just swallowed up the train. John downed his glass of champagne in one and poured himself another. He had already read the evening paper he had bought at the station from cover to cover, twice. The news was as bad as ever, apart from on the page dedicated to the exploits of the royal family. John let the paper slide onto the floor. This weekend in Paris was an excellent idea. He was really enjoying this champagne. A week had gone by since his last taste of the stuff, during the interval of the concert at the Royal Albert Hall. The adagio of Mahler's tenth symphony came into his head. The slow, sad movement of the music had got under John's skin on first hearing, and he had to admit that the sense of unease, almost sadness, it had stirred in him had stayed with him for the whole week, over the course of which he had listened to the passage several more times on his iPod. John had no particular interest in classical music. He preferred to listen to pop, sometimes jazz on nights out at piano bars. But on those occasions it was usually more about the person he was with than the music itself.

Chance had brought him to the Royal Albert Hall

that night. A friend, or rather a business contact, had been unable to go and had offered him his ticket. Chance sometimes arranged things rather well, John thought as he searched his bag for his iPod. Happening to meet someone you liked, happening upon a new piece of music: you never knew what might come of it. John had found out online that the symphony had been left unfinished. This struck him as rather poetic. The musician had been felled at the height of his career, mid-composition. Deep down, he thought, most of us would like to go the same way: in the prime of life. Old age blighted your existence with disease, impotence and dependency. People could be dead well before they actually kicked the bucket. On that note, what about that fuckwit who had come out of nowhere, fallen into him, collapsed in a heap, thrown up everywhere and wet himself? Instinctively, John sniffed the sleeve of his polo shirt. 'No. Don't think so. Can't smell anything. Imagine arriving in Paris smelling like crap. You'd be sent back at customs.' The idea made him smile. It had been a tough end to the day. The train had gathered pace once more, speeding along inside the cocoon of the tunnel. Everything was going well. John put his iPod down on the tray table in front of him. He wasn't sure he wanted to listen to the adagio again after all.

The carriage he was sitting in was only three-quarters full. The seat in front of him was occupied by a quiet young woman keeping herself to herself. She had not looked up from her laptop all journey. Out of curiosity or boredom, John leant over to try to see what she was so engrossed in. Might she be a secretary who had been forced to take work home with her? No, she was watching a film with her headphones in. The seat behind John's had been left vacant. Up ahead, the English couple had finally settled down. She appeared to have gone to sleep, and he would most likely do the same once he finished the can of beer he was holding limply in his hand. His arm dangled over the armrest. Soundlessly flying through the night, the carriage was like a haven of peace, a happy parenthesis from the chaos of everyday life. John was struggling to keep his eyes open. He was sipping his third glass of champagne. He knew sleep would soon envelop him and was enjoying putting off the moment as long as he could. His mind was wandering. Ali meant nothing to him. He behaved like a spoilt child, and John was sick of it. With Erbil, it had been another story.

Erbil was a young man, practically a boy, whom John had met back at the start of the summer, in early June. The encounter was to be a memorable one. Out on the pull in Soho, John had spotted a young, scruffy-looking guy lurking on the pavement opposite his regular hangout, The Duke of Edinburgh. The boy's haunting features and deep, dark eyes caught John's attention. There was a proud air about him, which made it difficult to watch him unnoticed. It was impossible to tell what kind of body he had, whether he was well built or not. When the boy's piercing gaze fell on John, it hit him like a body blow. He had gone inside the pub as much to escape the guy's unsettling presence as to get something to drink. Probably a rent boy, he thought to himself, sipping his first pint. That wasn't the kind of fun John was seeking. When he came back outside, the guy he'd had his eye on had gone. In spite of himself, John felt a pang of disappointment. Nevertheless, he brushed himself off and moved on to another bar. It wasn't until several hours later, when he was leaving a nightclub, that John caught sight of the boy again. Once again he was leaning against a wall like a cat on the prowl. Over the course of the night, John had repeatedly flirted and been flirted with, but he had moved on at the end of every dance. He left the club alone, worn out but still buzzing. Without a second's thought, he made a beeline for the boy he took to be a gigolo and offered him a cigarette as a conversation starter. The rest of the night was vivid in his memory. He had taken the young man home, washed him, fed him, given him too much to drink. Having got the boy half-cut, John had forced himself on him twice in succession, more carried away than he had been for ages. As he now replayed the images of that night, how he had entered the boy despite his protests, playing with his flimsy, drowsy body as though turning a matchbox over and over in his hands, kissing him full on the lips and grabbing the back of his neck to pull him closer, how he had finally made the boy come as he struggled against sleep – vivid, unshakeable images all the more violent for their fixation on the same few objects, the same parts of the body he had more or less raped (as he eventually admitted to himself a few days later, when he had ceased to act like an old rutting male); as he sank into this sexual reverie, rocked by the motion of the train, John was faced with the realisation that, three months down the line, he still felt the same burning desire to embrace that flesh.

His name was Erbil, or so he said. He came from Iraq and had entered England illegally, stowed away inside the fuel tank of an articulated lorry. He had paid top dollar for the privilege of this 'seat', and almost suffocated en route. But he had made it. He had succeeded, as he repeated often, beaming with childlike pride. Fate had been on his side. The lorry had got through the tunnel without being stopped. A few miles on, the driver had taken Erbil out of his hiding place and left him on the side of the road in the middle of nowhere. It was a beautiful day. Erbil saw England for the first time with the sun shining. He walked for a long time before hitching a lift with a couple from Brighton who were wise enough not to ask questions.

'So what now?' John had asked, torn between admiration and concern. Erbil dodged the question. They had gone on seeing one another almost every night for two weeks. Erbil would wait for John outside his flat in his habitual prowling cat pose. John would take him to dinner in a local trattoria; the kid was always starving. Having raced to finish their meal, they would head back to John's place and roll on top of one another, each desperate to rip the other's clothes off.

'Or was it only me who was mad about him?' wondered John. 'Maybe I projected my own feelings onto him. All I can say for sure is that I'd lost it.'

Several times John had tried to dig up more detail on his new lover's life, but Erbil was always evasive. He lived in north London with relatives – sometimes cousins, sometimes an uncle, it was a different story every time – worked all over the place, did odd jobs. One evening, John put his foot down and demanded to know his address, but the answer he squeezed out of Erbil was vague. It was somewhere near Arnos Grove, not far from Woodside Park. Erbil knew how to get there but not the exact address. John had flown into a rage and kicked him out.

The train was speeding along and all its passengers appeared to be asleep. 'After that, I stopped seeing him. And stopped thinking about him.' A few days after his outburst, John had consulted a map of Iraq, for fun, perhaps, or out of curiosity or nostalgia. Basra, Baghdad. Looking northwards, the name of a city made him sit up: Erbil. The little bastard had palmed him off with the name of some town. Everything else he had told John was probably a lie too. Erbil – John couldn't think what else to call him – claimed to have celebrated his eighteenth birthday soon after his arrival on British soil. It had suited John to believe him. He had no desire to be picked up by the police consorting with a minor, and an illegal immigrant at that. Yet when he stroked the boy's delicate skin, he knew perfectly well the kid could be no older than seventeen. Leaning his head against the window, John now thought it quite possible that Erbil had been under sixteen when he met him. He really was a kid. 'What could I have turned him into?'

The bottle of champagne had been empty for some time and the sandwich consumed without John even registering the fact. He had celebrated his forty-fifth birthday that August in Ibiza, accompanied by two guys he had met in London shortly beforehand. They had lived it up for a fortnight – eating out, going to clubs, having flings. Forty-five already, John thought to himself, sitting up straighter in his seat. He felt so old. He took out one of the two cans of beer he had stuffed into the pocket of the seat in front of him. He had just begun to sip it when the train slowed right down and lurched to a sudden halt. The fluorescent lights flickered and went out, plunging the carriage into darkness. A breakdown. This really wasn't John's day. He could hear raised voices around him. His fellow passengers were complaining about the lights. A Frenchman a few rows ahead cried foul. John's beer had gone warm. He put the can down on the tray and stretched out his legs. Now was the perfect time for a nap. John was exhausted. Suddenly he felt something pass around his neck.

'Fuck!' he barely had time to shout.

2

Juliette was laying the table for dinner. It had just gone eight o'clock and Roland was late, as usual. The children, Ludivine and Corentin, were watching a cartoon. It was the only thing Juliette could find to keep them quiet. The last few days' stormy weather and heavy atmosphere had been driving them up the wall. Wafts of the beef bourguignon bubbling on the stove were coming from the kitchen. It was a dish that could easily be reheated, she had told herself as she shopped, already anticipating that her husband would be held up at work. She had gone to buy the ingredients on her way home from the special school where she taught French. She liked her job, in spite of its challenges. While she waited in line at the butcher's, the sound of a police siren had taken her back ten years, to when she first met Roland.

It was chance that had thrown them together. Juliette was living in the tenth arrondissement at the time. One night, she had returned from the opera to find her flat had been burgled. Shock quickly gave way to panic and fear. She called the police, who told her to come and make a statement the following day or later in the week. Instead, she set off immediately, leaving the door to her flat wide open and falling off its hinges. She practically ran to the police station and arrived in a state of disarray, it having dawned on her en route that another thief might seize the opportunity to steal what little she had left: two pairs of jeans, three dresses and the bag she took to school. She was twenty-five and just starting out in her career. A junior officer took her into a small glass-walled room. It was past midnight and the man's tiredness was showing. He began tapping out Juliette's statement on an old typewriter in a perfunctory manner. Having expressed her surprise at the antiquated equipment – those were her exact words, 'Your equipment really is antiquated' – she met with a blank reaction and was forced to rephrase her remark, suddenly smiling and genial, having almost forgotten why she was there.

'That's some knackered old kit you've got there. I never thought I'd see one of those things again.'

Smiling half-heartedly, the officer replied weakly, 'The computer's broken.'

She was reeling off her name and address when a police lieutenant stuck his head round the door to have a word with the officer. She heard his voice before she saw his face; its tone was warm but firm. He was asking for a report that his subordinate had not yet finished. While the officer mumbled his excuses, Juliette turned round to look at the man he was speaking to. He was standing right behind her, almost touching her. Flustered, unprepared for the encounter, she straightened in her chair. Looking up at him, she met his gaze searing deep into her eyes. And then he was gone. Under interrogation by Juliette, the junior officer told her the man in question was Lieutenant Desfeuillères. She made her way home soon afterwards feeling strange, wondering if she had imagined that voice and the look he had given her, which she couldn't get out of her mind. Nothing else about him had stood out. If someone had asked her to describe what he looked like, she wouldn't have known where to start.

'What can I get you?'

The butcher shook her from her daydream. She stammered two or three words before pulling herself together.

'I'll have eight hundred grams of stewing steak, please.'

The young man behind the counter, who could barely be eighteen, had not been working there long. He had a nice manner with the customers and took his role seriously. He made Juliette laugh; he was a joker. He could have been one of her students. She had only been served by him two or three times when he started trying to flirt with her, but he did the same to everybody.

'Looking gorgeous today, Madame.' After the second time he told her his name: 'I'm Mohamed.'

'Anything else for you?'

Le flic. Nowadays she called Roland 'the cop'. The junior officer had warned her that burglars were very rarely caught. There was no need for her to come back to the station. They would write if there was any news. Nevertheless two weeks later, naturally having heard nothing, Juliette returned 'just on the off-chance', as she told the officer manning the front desk. He was preparing to turn her away when Lieutenant Desfeuillères appeared. If chance had brought them together the first time, their next encounter could only be the work of fate. The lieutenant recognised Juliette at once and invited her into his office.

'I'll look after Madame,' he told the officer. And the rest was history.

It was after nine when Juliette heard the key turn in the door. By now she was furious. The children had eaten. She was on the verge of putting them to bed, but knew how much Roland loved to be welcomed home by them. The sight of the two kids running at his legs instantly made him happy.

'Bedtime!' Juliette announced emphatically, in a tone that admitted no protest. However, the soon to be nine-year-old Ludivine was intent on staying up to give her father a goodnight kiss.

'He doesn't care!' Juliette spat without thinking.

Before she knew it, Ludivine was in tears. Her younger brother took advantage of the distraction to race towards the front door.

'Papa!'

Ludivine scurried after him, her tears suddenly dried and her face lit up.

'Did you find the murderer? Go on, tell me, Papa!' the little boy asked, while his sister let herself be scooped up in the arms she would have liked all to herself. 'Do you still love me?'

The children went off to bed, taking their excitement with them. The apartment felt quiet and empty in their absence. Juliette was at the end of her tether. She no longer found the kids' nightly performance amusing. She picked a book off the shelves at random and made for the living room. Passing her husband, she nodded towards the kitchen.

'There's a beef bourguignon on the stove. Serve yourself.'

Roland grabbed her by the arm.

'Aren't you going to give me a kiss?'

Juliette dropped the book.

'Stop it.'

Roland wouldn't let go. He tried to pull her towards him for a hug. She held back.

'Let go.'

Her face dropped. She looked up at her husband, afraid. He suddenly realised what was going through her mind. He had seen so many battered wives at the station. He was overcome by a mixture of shame and anger. How could she believe such a thing? He had never even raised his voice at her let alone dreamt of raising a hand to her. Something between them had just snapped. They both felt it without yet understanding it. Roland pulled his hand away sharply, as if he had accidentally touched a scorching hotplate. His tiredness was written on his face; it had been a long day, which had started early.

He had sweated in his suit. The slight bulge of a burgeoning gut showed through the damp white shirt. He got away with carrying a bit of extra weight because he was tall: six foot, and proud of it. He was, or rather had been a good-looking man in his day. Now only his black hair seemed to have escaped the ravages of age. Tonight it was messy and greasy. Juliette couldn't help passing a critical eye over the man she had been so in love with, and wished she could love still. She no longer saw in the cop who stood before her the sexy, self-assured man who had taken her into his office ten years earlier. 'How can I help?' he had asked with a smile on his lips and that warm voice she had come back to hear again.

Juliette picked her book off the floor without a word. He watched her cross the corridor. She was still beautiful. It was only the way she acted that had become a bit stiff. Sometimes, like tonight, she played this cross, schoolmarmish part that Roland couldn't stand. The day they met, he had first seen her from behind. Her long, curly brown hair fell onto the bare skin at the top of her back. Juliette had just got back from a performance of *Tristan and Isolde* at the Opéra Bastille. She was wearing a simple, elegant short-sleeved black dress which showed off the shape of her back. That was the image of her that stayed with Roland for a long time afterwards: hair tumbling onto a perfectly straight back in a close-fitting evening gown. When she looked over her shoulder at him, he had been struck by the intensity of her green eyes meeting his gaze. They had often reminisced about that moment. Juliette spoke of the 'captive stares' they had exchanged, and her turn of phrase had lingered in Roland's mind as much as the memory of the moment itself.

Roland really couldn't face an argument tonight. He had only just left a crime scene. No matter how used he was to seeing dead bodies, they still left him shaken, and he wasn't prepared for coming home to a fight. He hung in the corridor, incapable of making a decision. Not today, not now, he kept telling himself. Not that there was ever a good time for a domestic. Unless you were gunning for an argument, that was, and had laid the ground, brought it about on purpose. Picking a fight as a way out. At first, the thought made him shudder, but a second later he was smiling slyly. Not now. By this point he just felt confused and weak. He wasn't really hungry.

What had possessed Juliette to make beef bourguignon in this heat? The smells coming out of the kitchen made him gag. He couldn't stop thinking about the case he had been attending to less than an hour earlier.

A decapitated body had been found in a rubbish container. The stench had alerted people nearby. For the last three days, a refuse collectors' strike had been blighting the streets of Paris. The city's bins were overflowing. Hundreds of bags of rubbish were piled up on pavements. Rats had been spotted. Buried under the mountain of waste lay the torso of a young black man. He must have been there for a couple of days. A kid of sixteen or seventeen, judging by his frame. The body had been stripped naked. The police had gone through all the junk without finding the slightest piece of evidence. Decapitations don't happen every day. Cutting off a man's head isn't easy. The neck is strong. You need the right tools, the right knowledge and, of course, the will to do it, which is to say one heck of a motive. As he recorded the details of the scene before him – the exact location of the container on Boulevard Magenta, the number of bin bags it held (ninety-five), the position and state of the body – Lieutenant Desfeuillères mulled it all over. A mafia hit, a dispute over drugs that had gone missing, perhaps, or been sold to the wrong person. Maybe the kid had tried to go it alone and had been busted, in the nastiest possible way. Forensics turned up soon after Roland, taking photographs, checking for fingerprints. The body was inspected from every angle before being sent to the coroner. Roland signed his report and made a run for it, feeling sick at what he had just seen. It was after 8.30 p.m. when he left. By the time he got back to the twentieth arrondissement, the kids would be in bed and Juliette would be fuming. Roland hadn't had a chance to let her know he would be late. He had got the call to attend the scene while he was packing up for the day, eager to get home to his wife. The beat officer who had rung him had sounded so panicked that the lieutenant had reacted in the same way.

'I found the headless body of a tall black man inside a rubbish container.'

'Shit!' Roland blurted. 'On my way.'

At what point could he possibly have rung his wife?

Now he was standing with his arms dangling by his sides in the gloom of the corridor, which the light from the living room did little to lift. What a stupid argument about nothing. Roland was on the verge of turning round and leaving. But where to? Neither could he face going into the living room to be glared at. What am I doing here? Some part of him was on its way out. He knew neither which part, nor where it was going. It was like water leaking from a burst pipe. He suddenly pictured a whirlpool. He saw himself trying to swim against the current, being sucked towards an enormous plughole. Then, for no apparent reason, this image led on to another, perhaps to counteract it: a nice shower, which would make him feel better again.

Roland tiptoed into the bathroom to avoid waking the children. The sight of his own face in the mirror gave him a fright. His features were drawn. The stubbly chin and greasy hair made him appear five years older. He looked awful. He slapped his cheeks. 1) Shave; 2) shower: wash hair and have a rub-down; 3) dry off, moisturise, slap on some after-shave lotion. No. Cologne. Juliette's most recent gift to him. He wanted to smell nice for her, win her round. Twenty minutes later, Roland stood facing the mirror again. He admired himself, pleased with the results of his efforts. He was peering more closely at his skin when the memory of the torso-man returned, putting an abrupt end to the brief spell of satisfaction. It was shaping up to be a difficult inquiry. The person, or rather persons, who had committed the murder – they were definitely murderers in the plural – the crazy bastards who had cut the kid's head off were no amateurs. Roland hoped someone else would be put in charge of the case. He had only just wrapped up a delicate fraud investigation involving a number of celebrities. He had tackled the job sensitively and with the utmost discretion. Only two names had got out into the press. He had been congratulated by the public prosecutor. Nice work. Roland looked up. He was smiling again. It was the start of a quiet weekend. He was looking forward to spending time with his children and his wife. It was time he went to find her.

Dressed in a new pair of jeans and a white shirt, Roland made his entrance into the living room like an actor embarking on his debut performance. He had stage fright. Juliette had put her book down at her feet. She was curled up in the armchair looking determinedly relaxed. The halogen lamp cast a warm glow. A Gustav Mahler concert was playing on the radio that Friday, live from the Royal Albert Hall. Stopping to listen, Roland recognised the piece as the Austrian composer's symphony Juliette had put on almost every night for the last few months. The music, which Roland found boring, helped her unwind after work, she said. The storm seemed to have passed. Roland hesitated, seized with a feeling of doubt as he looked around the room, closely scrutinising the place they had called home for the past five years. The white walls of the living room had greyed over time. The red sofa had faded, as had the canary yellow armchairs which Juliette had bought to liven up the room. And Juliette herself was perhaps not as beautiful now as Roland wanted to believe she was. Still feeling unsure of himself, stumbling over his lines, he found himself thinking it was about time they gave the living room a fresh lick of paint, and a new set of furniture wouldn't be a bad idea either.

'Hello, anybody home?' asked Juliette, level-voiced.

'It's lovely, what you're listening to. I haven't heard this part before,' he replied, trying to sound interested.

The brass section tutti of Mahler's tenth suddenly blasted out. 'Great,' thought the lieutenant. 'Here come the trumpeters of doom.'

'Aren't you going to eat something?'

'I'm not really hungry. I've had a bit of a day of it. Shall we have a whisky?'

The storm was far off now. If Juliette agreed to this drink, it meant there was light on the horizon. She didn't jump at the offer.

'I promised myself I wouldn't drink today.'

'On a Friday night?' Roland asked incredulously.

He moved closer, gently placing a hand on her shoulder.

'Alright, just the one.'

She was backing down.

'Tell me about your day,' she finally said.

The following Friday 19 September, Juliette booked a babysitter for the evening. Roland had asked her out for dinner. Juliette agreed without displaying much enthusiasm, but the truth was she was pleased. It was about time her husband tried to patch things up. Roland had been thinking the same thing. He felt it was his job to sort things out. Going for a meal seemed a good solution. He had chosen a nice restaurant in the seventh arrondissement.

Roland had booked a table for nine o'clock, anticipating he might be late leaving work. As luck would have it, he had only minor matters to deal with that day: break-ins, pickpocketing, fights between junkies at Gare du Nord, credit card fraud and so on. The mystery of the torso-man had been entrusted to one of his colleagues. So in fact Roland arrived home early to find Juliette in the bath. 'It worked!' he concluded at once. 'She's making an effort. We're back in business!' He kissed her neck, complimenting her on the softness of her skin, to demonstrate his desire to win back her affection. She had had an exhausting day. A class of twelve-year-olds she thought she had under control had turned against her. She couldn't understand why. Was she incompetent? 'Not just at school, I mean, but generally.'

'Do you still love me?'

The question caught Roland off-guard. He had been expecting it, hoping for it even, but later – at the end of the meal, for example. He chose to reply with a kiss. Juliette waved him away, smiling.

'Not now.'

When Juliette had finished in the bathroom, Roland took a quick shower. Cleanly shaven, combed and cologned, he put on a navy blue shirt over a clean pair of jeans. 'A bit hello-sailor. But, hey, blue does suit me.'

Juliette was waiting for him in the living room, going over her instructions to the babysitter. Absolutely no sweets. TV off at nine. The girl nodded silently. She was intimidated by Juliette's elegant appearance.

Juliette had decided to wear black, perhaps in homage to the famous dress she had been wearing the night she met Roland. Her first thought had been to go for a simple T-shirt, worn without a bra. 'I can still get away with it,' she had told herself, running her hands over her breasts in front of the bedroom mirror. Then, less confidently, she had felt her stomach. There was no use lying to herself. It wasn't flat anymore. 'I'll look ridiculous in a tight-fitting top. I'll bulge out of it. Better not.' She put the T-shirt back in the cupboard. She might just about be able to wear it on holiday. Or perhaps she should get back to the gym. But when would she find the time? She pored over every inch of her body, as if it belonged to another woman. She had put on a few pounds. Not much. She wasn't overweight. Just a bit of flab. Her body was just tired. She smiled at her own words. That was it, spot on, exactly the right way to describe it; but try telling that to the cop. Roland didn't look at her enough. She had let herself go because he wanted her less. Did he want her at all? Juliette brushed away the question. Thankfully her legs were still in good shape. She had always been proud of her long, slender legs. Gazelle legs. Where had she read that? In *The One Thousand and One Nights*? The image cropped up all over the place. So skinny jeans it was, a well-cut black pair. They would have gone well with the black top which she had taken back out of the cupboard for another look. But no, she really couldn't. The question of shoes was solved on the spot. Espadrilles. Sporty, elegant and relaxed, all at once. Perfect for the occasion. Juliette would never have dreamed of wearing heels. She didn't need the added height since she was already six foot tall, plus she thought stilettos looked common. So now for the top half. A black shirt didn't work with black jeans; a T-shirt, yes, a shirt, no. It was too much. Too prim and proper. She wasn't sure why but she knew instinctively it would make her look frumpy. The blue one was a no-no too. Juliette suspected that Roland would be wearing the blue shirt she had bought him. Yet she wasn't exactly spoilt for choice. The rail was hung with a sad selection of shirts and skirts she never wore. She didn't have much of a wardrobe. Thanks to her job, she had gradually come to wear pretty much the same thing all the time: low-key, functional outfits. Juliette rarely wore make-up. Age had begun to make her care less about looking good. Her husband's disinterest had done the rest. Tonight, she felt newly aware of her own femininity. She was grateful to Roland for that. Being asked out for dinner at a smart restaurant forced her to learn the art of seduction again, like being sent back to school. The next minute she felt a pang of resentment for the fact he had taken so long about it. She wasn't sure she wanted to be a schoolgirl again. 'What game are we playing with one another?' she asked herself. She didn't have the answer. This red silk blouse was the one. She had bought it on a whim a year earlier at

Bon Marché, when she had been in the mood for an impulsive purchase. She had never worn it. Too red, too showy. Maybe tonight was the night to stand out. Juliette wanted to be looked at. Her brown hair, almost as long now as it had been when they met, was tumbling in an artful mess over her shiny blouse when Roland found her talking to the babysitter in the living room. He couldn't help but think to himself that Juliette had not so much got dressed as got into costume. 'We shall go to the ball,' he said to himself. Juliette had caught the look of surprise on her husband's face and been seized with doubt, but brushed the feeling aside. The blue shirt. 'I knew it,' she told herself, examining Roland in turn.

Desfeuillères had come home from the station early, leaving his new deputy, Sub-lieutenant Bouallem, in charge. Originally from Marseilles, Samy Bouallem had been transferred to Paris in early summer. Having just turned thirty-five, he was younger than his boss, and had his sights set on moving up the ranks. Dynamic as well as thorough, he had very quickly become invaluable to Desfeuillères. The two men got on well and often had lunch together.

Roland therefore had no qualms at all about leaving work a bit before time. He had to pick something up before going home, something important. It was a purchase he had been contemplating for some time, ever since two of his colleagues had put the idea in his head. One had told him it was fashionable, the other that everybody had one. Despite having hit forty, the lieutenant wasn't all that worldly wise. He had only ever been with one woman, and had never been tempted to cheat on Juliette. As their sex life had dwindled both in frequency and quality, Juliette had on more than one occasion faked an orgasm; her husband had not been fooled. Roland had 1) told himself these things happen over time; 2) wondered if a dip in your sex life could break up a marriage; 3) decided to be more attentive to his wife. This simple chain of thoughts had taken a good few weeks to formulate. The events of the previous weekend had persuaded him to bring forward his plan. Lying awake in the middle of the night, he had put his thoughts in order: 1) time, 2) sexuality, 3) desire. Or was it 1) sex, 2) the years passing? No, he told himself as his eyelids grew steadily heavier, no one fucks the same way at forty as they did at eighteen. So time came top. Having to endure his colleagues' teasing had allowed him to see his relationship troubles in perspective.

'You need to win her back,' said one. 'Surprise her,' added another.

The problem, as is so often the case, lay in deciding how to go about it. A dirty weekend just wasn't going to cut it.

'Too easy, too obvious,' threw in the younger of his colleagues. 'Teenage tactics,' the other mocked.

Desfeuillères sat in uncomfortable silence.

'You know what you have to do...'

The lieutenant normally did his best to avoid this kind of conversation, but the fear of losing Juliette had weakened his defences. We often tell ourselves (only to take it back straight afterwards) that we can learn from others, that deep down we're all bogged down in the same issues, the same miserable existence that catches us all in the end. So, what are you going to do about it?

As he left the station, Roland had been on the brink of telling his sub-lieutenant the reason behind his rush, but thought better of it. In spite of Samy's warm and friendly manner, there was sometimes an austere expression on his face which suggested a puritanical streak. Best not to say anything. He was still young. Having arrived outside the sex shop, Roland dived in like a thief afraid of being caught in the act.

He and Juliette were now sitting face to face across the table. Elegantly laid though it was, with damask tablecloth and napkins, porcelain dishes, crystal glasses and silver candlesticks, its location was awful. Juliette and Roland had been seated at the back of the restaurant, close to the toilets.

'How lovely,' remarked Juliette, who immediately asked to move to another table.

The waiter, a young Asian man with a curious manner, waved his hand at the packed dining room by way of response before scarpering, leaving their menus on the table in front of them. Roland suggested ordering a glass of champagne, a notion immediately shot down by Juliette. She felt ridiculous in her red silk blouse. Walking into the restaurant, she had glanced around at what the other women were wearing; it didn't take long to realise scarlet was out of fashion. Everyone was in pink. When the waiter showed them to their outlying table, Juliette told herself it was no wonder they were putting her in the corner. 'I look like a peasant in my Sunday best,' she thought. A glass of champagne would have been the icing on the cake. They might as well be living in the provinces. Juliette belonged to a family of boho Belleville artisans. Roland was from Brittany. He had grown up in the town of Lorient, a fact she could not resist reminding him of.

'This is just like one of those Relais & Châteaux places in your village.'

'It's not in the bag yet,' thought Roland, choosing to remain silent. Playing the smooth cop, he waved authoritatively at the waiter, who hurried over.

'I'll have a whisky. What do you want?' he asked, staring hard at his wife.

'The same,' she told the waiter.

'One—nil,' thought the lieutenant. He felt relaxed. He was comfortable in his sailor kit. It hadn't crossed his mind to even glimpse at what anyone else was wearing. Like all headstrong people, Roland saw everything he started right through to the end. This pig-headedness could sometimes evolve into self-delusion, and from there to catastrophe. Tonight he was heading for disaster. As far as Juliette was concerned, the night was hanging in the balance. She was waiting, though for what, she wasn't sure. A stroke of magic, probably; a miracle, in other words. 'Is he going to get a handle on this?' she asked herself as she peered over her menu at her husband, who was making a show of studying his. 'I'll hand it to him, he came back well on the whisky. But now what?'

By the time the waiter delivered the coffees, Juliette was beginning to enjoy herself. She and Roland had both ordered the chef's special, the Oriental-style pigeon. They had drunk an excellent Pommard which had started to go to their heads. Several times during the night, between the starter and main course and again between the pigeon and dessert, Roland had stroked his wife's hand. As they moved on to the final dish, an orange soufflé accompanied by a glass of syrupy dessert wine, the ice was finally broken. From the whisky right up until the theatrical arrival of the soufflé, the talk had been strained and excessively polite. Each of them knew that the occasion demanded a certain level of conversation, a turn of phrase in line with the glamorous setting: ideas and feelings in the Relais & Châteaux mould. Yet it also struck both of them that they had no more to say to one another here than they did eating together at home.

It was the celebratory feel and amusing appearance

of that marvel, the soufflé, a kind of hot-air balloon of patisserie flying against the laws of gravity, that finally made them relax and enjoy each other's company. It was also the signal that dinner was almost over. They took it as the cue to finally open up to one another. Roland said he was sorry for what he had done the previous Friday, when he had grabbed Juliette's arm in a manner she had found threatening, though he hadn't meant it that way.

'I was knackered. It was the end of a long day. I just needed a hug.'

Juliette conceded she had overreacted to what was after all just one false move. Then they had gone further back into their shared history, admitting other mistakes they had each made, things they had forgotten, and reliving the high points too. They had always been there for each other. The children had come along. Their two darlings. A stroke of luck? 'Love,' said Juliette. Shit, yes, the children. The babysitter was booked until midnight. Juliette checked her watch. They had just under half an hour to get back to the twentieth arrondissement. She thought she ought to warn the girl, 'We might be a little late.' Meanwhile Roland settled the bill, glancing at his mobile phone. His deputy had sent him a message.

'Busy night. Messy situation, but we're handling it. Would rather be in a restaurant. Samy.'

Intrigued, Roland was about to call him when the waiter arrived to tell them their taxi had just pulled up outside.

*

The sex toy lay dormant inside its hard, transparent plastic case. Under the bed, it waited to be turned on and sent into sweaty battle. It seemed to have a life of its own, like a kind of mythical creature. Roland hadn't known where else to hide the thing, which embarrassed and fascinated him in equal measure.

Meanwhile Juliette was busy thanking the babysitter and offering her an hour's extra pay for the additional ten minutes' work their late return had caused her. As he listened to his wife, full of admiration for her good nature, Roland wondered how best to present her with his find. Was it something that needed to be talked about first, or should he just grab it on the spur of the moment? He couldn't help smiling. The toy, a simple vibrator, had turned him on in the shop, but now he wasn't so sure. He probably should have put it back on the shelf with all the other oddities, but Roland had decided to go through with it. 'What's the worst that can happen? I'll get a slap or she'll laugh in my face. Otherwise, I'll never know. My own wife is a mystery to me. What does she like? This filthy thing's making me hard. Why doesn't she do that to me?'

'I'll go and check on the children,' he told Juliette, slipping out of the room.

The sex toy hadn't moved an inch. It was sitting quietly under the bed, exactly where Roland had left it several hours earlier. 'I'm an idiot,' he told himself, carefully taking it into his hands. He could hear snippets of the conversation going on at the other end of the corridor. The two women were still talking. Roland took the toy out of its packaging and looked at it closely. It was cold and hard, not very pretty, merely suggestive. The appliance was battery-operated. Luckily the woman on the till had pointed this out to Roland. The thing didn't just vibrate of its own accord. 'Can't go expecting miracles,' he was thinking as he listened to her. How had she come to this career? She handled the gadgets on offer in her shop with the professional air of a saleswoman at Galeries Lafayette. It wasn't very hard to figure out. Roland inserted the four batteries into the back of the vibrator and tested it. *Vrrr... Vrrr...* It worked just fine; it purred. Soon it would pounce. An image flashed through Roland's mind as he let his hand stroke up and down the toy. 'It's powered by the thunder of God,' he said to himself, a sizeable erection straining the fabric of his trousers. At the sound of the front door opening, he put the vibrator back under the bed, ready for use. As he walked back into the living room, he was imagining making Juliette come with the sex toy. Tonight, he was determined to bring her to the peak of pleasure.

She was on edge. She had barely closed the door on the babysitter when Roland was all over her, kissing her full on the mouth before she had time to draw breath.

'What about the children?' she said, freeing herself from his grasp.

'They're fast asleep.'

Roland was already wrapping his arms back around Juliette, unbuttoning her blouse, grasping at her breasts so he could finally press his skin against hers. It was all a bit much for Juliette. She needed another drink before she could let herself go. They hadn't had sex for a month, maybe longer. She pushed Roland away gently but firmly.

'Not so fast,' she said, affecting outrage to keep him on his toes.

She wished she could remember when and where they had last done it. Not at home – she was certain of that. Roland followed her into the living room. He grabbed her like a ragdoll around the waist and ran his hands over her hips. She was on the verge of giving him a slap. She wriggled free, more forcefully this time. It was sinking in that she didn't feel any desire for him, at least not right now or like this.

Actually, it was here, after all. The memory suddenly came back to her. Five weeks earlier, during the summer holidays. A couple of friends had come round for dinner. The kids were staying with their grandparents out in the country. It was a great night. They all stayed up drinking until the small hours. When their friends left at around four in the morning, she and Roland were a bit tipsy. Nevertheless they had one last drink, because they felt like it, because it was a bit naughty, because they were making the most of the total freedom that the absence of their children opened up to them. In bed, Roland humped her like a rabbit. It wasn't very good. He came quickly and fell asleep. She passed out soon afterwards, knocked out by the alcohol. An hour later the sunrise woke her with a start.

Roland wouldn't let go of her. She went to sit down, or rather slump, into one of the egg-yolk-yellow armchairs they had bought back when life was good, but he grabbed her by the hand.

'Don't you want to?' he asked slightly gruffly, impatient to get started and beginning to worry it wasn't going to happen.

Moments later he had her pinned against the wall. She thought of claiming to have a headache, but then she would have to pass on the glass of whisky she was still hankering after. She needed a shot of something strong. She could have explained to him that she just wanted to relax first, and afterwards ... But she knew there would be no afterwards tonight. She just didn't feel like it. Not that the meal hadn't gone well. They had had a good long talk and recovered some of their closeness. But now her husband seemed like a stranger. She felt trapped. 'I'm stuck,' she thought as she pushed away her husband's hand.

'We don't have to, you know.' She had uttered the words gently, tenderly, almost lovingly. They sounded hollow. Roland stepped right back into the second armchair, which he sank into without a further thought.

He bowed his head and stared at the armrest. The piss-yellow fabric made him feel sick.

'Right. So what now?'

Juliette went off to bed without answering. She no longer had the energy to pour herself a drink. She no longer felt like relaxing. She no longer had the strength to start a fight. All she wanted to do was sleep.

As she got undressed, she noticed something under the bed. To begin with, she thought it must be one of Ludivine's dolls. Her daughter liked coming to play in their room. Juliette knelt down and reached for the child's forgotten plaything. She was already envisaging telling Ludivine off the next morning. She could not have been more surprised. Juliette had never held a sex toy in her hands before. She must have seen one, she supposed. But she had certainly never spoken of such a thing. It wasn't the kind of topic that came up in the school canteen over lunch with her colleagues. The thing fell almost straight out of her hands. 'The slut!' Juliette's suspicions pointed straight to the young babysitter. She was knocked for six. She had left her children in the care of a girl who had devoted all her attention to masturbating. Juliette felt panic rising. What if the children had seen her, or heard her at it? The television was in the living room. The girl had probably put on a pornographic film. 'The slut,' she said again, red with rage. She stormed into the living room semi-naked, clutching the vibrator in her hand.

Roland was sipping a whisky when he caught sight of his wife, misconstruing her heated appearance entirely. Standing in her knickers, breasts bared and face flushed, she brandished the sex toy like a flag. Roland stood up like a shot, as blown away as Juliette. She was about to speak when he took her in his arms, cutting off the unnecessary explanations. 'Score,' he said to himself. He smacked his lips against hers, taking the sex toy out of her hand to press it against her buttocks. She shoved him away.

'Are you out of your mind?' she hissed, pushing aside the vibrator. 'That slut has already done enough harm bringing that piece of filth into the house.'

'What are you talking about?' asked Roland. 'What does anyone else have to do with it?'

Juliette stood speechless, keeping a good distance from her husband. Either she didn't understand or was refusing to grasp what he was hinting at. So he spelled out exactly when and how he had bought the toy, his embarrassment, the advice of the saleswoman, the funny side of the situation, come on, you're a French teacher after all, you should know why I bought it, to get close to you, to spice things up a bit. His voice trailed off, silenced by Juliette's icy glare. She hated him. Her silence unhinged him.

'Don't go acting disgusted with me! You know how it is. You weren't born yesterday.' He had raised his voice.

She yelled back at him, 'Bastard.'

The argument that had been brewing for months had finally broken out. Each blamed the other for the breakdown of their marriage.

'You really are a stupid fuck,' spat Juliette.

'And you're a sour old cow who can't get over her shitty little job.'

He was yelling too. That's when the children appeared, sleepy and puffy-eyed.

'What's going on?' asked Corentin. 'Why are you shouting?'

'What's that?' asked Ludivine, pointing to the sex toy in her father's hand.

3

23.30. The London to Paris train had just arrived, ten minutes late.

As soon as the doors unlocked, passengers began to leave the train in groups of two or three. There was a certain amount of shoving and grumbling. Everyone wanted to be the first off. In a few minutes the platform reserved for the cross-Channel train was rammed with hurrying passengers, their suitcases on wheels wobbling along behind them. Some had immediately lit cigarettes, the smoking ban having made that even more attractive, others were sending texts. Younger passengers, their bags slung across their shoulders, were racing for the exit under the impassive eye of the cleaners who were chatting as they waited for the human tide to recede before boarding the train to remove the detritus of the journey.

'Wake up! Wake up!'

In one of the two first class carriages at the front of the train, Mr Lewis was trying to wake one of his compatriots still dozing in his seat.

'Come on now, wake up!' he repeated without success.

The other first class passengers had left the carriage. No one apart from Mr Lewis and his wife, Margaret, had paid any attention to the wino whose deep slumber seemed the inevitable and predictable result of the bottles of champagne and beer heaped at his feet. Philip Lewis was the only one to have taken pity on the solitary passenger, probably because he remembered being in a similar state after pub crawling in Fulham after a football match. At first his wife had tried to dissuade him from his generous impulse. She was tired. She was worried that their hotel, although pre-booked, wouldn't keep their room after midnight. Philip hadn't listened to her.

'Wake up now!'

Margaret pulled her husband by the elbow. 'He's completely sozzled,' she remarked matter-of-factly. She had seen them before and knew that nothing could be done for him. The poor thing was not moving an inch. His chest was still. 'That's not normal,' objected Philip. 'Wake up!'

Finally, Philip took the step of putting a hand on his compatriot's shoulder. He was cold. 'Leave it,' exclaimed Margaret, 'he's going to get us into trouble. Come on!' But Philip persisted. He gave the man's shoulder a light tap. His motionless body immediately toppled against the armrest revealing a purplish mark around his neck.

Margaret uttered a cry of fright. Philip couldn't hold back his 'Fuck!' They were stuck with a dead body, and the body had a worrying aspect. 'Murder?' asked Mrs Lewis, speaking to herself as much as to her husband. She had been all for leaving the train, Philip's sense of duty had restrained them. Now he pointed out, to justify himself, that they would be the prime suspects if they were caught trying to flee the scene. His wife could see that. They needed help. But who was there to ask?

Two cleaners were calmly smoking a cigarette on the platform. Most of the passengers had left the station but there was still a group of about thirty Chinese tourists in front of one of the standard class carriages. They were loudly discussing, some were shouting, others were gesticulating. Perhaps someone had stolen one of their bags. They were amusing the cleaners, Abdou and Salim, who were watching them surreptitiously, and mimicking them by narrowing their eyes and pulling their heads into their necks.

'Excuse me?'

Abdou and Salim greeted Philip's request with exaggerated irritation. He was interrupting them. He asked them for help in his bad French. One of his countrymen was in a very bad way in one of the first class carriages, which Philip pointed out. Prudently Philip did not mention that the man was dead. Abdou had turned to his mate. No idea what this Englisher is going on about. Salim who had worked for more than two years for the cross-Channel company explained to Abdou that the trains arriving from London were always a complete mess. Every time you had to pick up hundreds of empty bottles, clean the spillage in the toilets, not to mention the drunks you had to take by the scruff of the neck and throw off the train. 'That's disgusting!' said Abdou looking disapprovingly at Philip before turning his back on him. Philip couldn't understand what the two men said, but he saw that they didn't believe him. So he risked everything and was careful to make himself clear. 'There's a dead man on the train.' The two men laughed, 'Dead drunk, you mean!' They turned away, taking their dustpans and brushes with them. Philip was about to call after them when he heard his wife.

Margaret came slowly, buttoned in her pink suit, dragging behind her two little suitcases on wheels. She was sweating. She explained to her husband that she couldn't stand to spend another minute with the dead body. He quickly told her how the cleaners had been no help.

'Let's go to the police,' she said.

'Are you sure you haven't left anything in the compartment?' asked her husband, vaguely worried.

'No. There was nothing apart from the body.'

Margaret's mood had changed. Her feeling of exhaustion when faced with the dead body had been replaced by a feeling of excitement close to euphoria.

Now she was finding it all very interesting. Her husband and she were probably the only witnesses to the murder. Philip corrected her. They hadn't witnessed the murder, all they had done was find the body. Philip could well imagine the questions the police would ask them. He started to sweat himself as he saw the moment he would sit down to a nice pint of beer receding into the distance. He was growing weary of this death and would happily have swapped the body for a Guinness. Margaret was not at all of that opinion. Her husband was failing to see the positives of the situation and she set about putting him right. The press would want to speak to them. Definitely. Their photograph would be on the front page of the *Sun*. They would be recognised in the street. Philip shrugged. He wasn't in the mood. But Margaret had another winning argument. 'Think of the effect on your business!' she said, with the air of one who knows a thing or two about business. Her husband owned a prosperous discount furniture shop in Fulham that sold natural pine beds, MDF wardrobes, sofa-beds and acrylic sofas. The banner over the shop entrance declared 'everything for home comfort'. And Margaret pressed on, 'We'll get lots of new customers.' Philip nodded. His other half was right. He pictured the till ringing merrily. 'Let's go and find the police,' he said.

Their machine guns slung across them, two military policemen were patrolling the concourse of Gare du

Nord. They were both tall and well-built, their biceps straining their uniforms, which identified them from afar. Philip and Margaret dashed towards them, hot and out of breath. The officers immediately grabbed their weapons and pointed them at the pair.

'Woah!' exclaimed Philip.

'Oh my God,' was Margaret's reaction.

They stopped short a few paces from the policemen.

'Move on!' barked Robert Lalumière.

'Clear off!' clarified the more junior of the two, Émile Dupuy.

But it was going to take more than that to dissuade Margaret, who immediately begged her husband to let her speak to them. She was finding it all increasingly exciting. 'We'll be on the front page,' she repeated, her eyes wide with anticipation. Philip said not a word. He was frightened.

'Gentlemen, we have a problem. There's a man in the carriage and …'

Margaret was struggling to speak French. Lalumière did not allow her to continue.

'Move along!' he repeated.

Philip dared to take a step forward. 'Gentlemen! A man is dead in that carriage!'

Dupuy waved his machine gun left and right to illustrate his words: 'We've asked you to clear off.'

Philip was now sweating freely. His Chelsea top showed sweat patches not just under his arms, but also across his potbelly and at the back of his neck. His legs turned to jelly. After stepping back, he tried one last time, 'There's a murdered man on the train.'

Dupuy, ignoring the remark and the man, remarked to his colleague, 'Drunk, like the Irish.'

Lalumière burst out laughing, and sticking the barrel of his machine gun into Mr Lewis's stomach, said, 'Clear off!'

'We'd better leave it,' said Philip to his wife.

They had not gone far when they heard a man yelling at them. Philip turned round, his face ashen as he took in one of the two military policemen running straight at him. Philip had a sudden moment of clarity. Margaret was right. They were the only witnesses to the murder. He seized his wife's hand and dragged her towards the exit. 'Run!'

Now he was definitely set on getting out of there and God willing, settling down somewhere far away with a pint. But he only half believed in that possibility, just as he only half believed in God. As midnight struck, he felt a powerful hand grab his arm, forcing him to let go of his suitcase on wheels. 'This is the end,' he thought, not trying to offer any resistance as they put the handcuffs on. Margaret on the other hand was less compliant. She fought when Dupuy tried to get hold of her. As he was pulling her towards him, she began to shriek, 'This is outrageous. You've no right.' As she struggled, she thrust her hands into her suit pockets so that the policeman could not get the cuffs on her. A little crowd was gathering round them. Still struggling, Margaret was pleased to note that more and more people seemed interested. She was causing a scandal. And she was sure the press would soon be on the scene. She shouted louder. Philip was decidedly less enthusiastic. In his handcuffs, he immediately felt guilty. He would have liked to escape the gaze of the onlookers. Besides they didn't look very appetising. At this late hour, it wasn't exactly celebrities who were hanging around Gare du Nord. A few tramps, their hands in their pockets, cigarettes hanging from their mouths, had stopped to watch what was going on, more because they had nothing better to do, than from any real curiosity. Three stoned youths were regarding Margaret's shrieking with amusement, perhaps wondering if she had dropped some acid. The other onlookers were suburbanites momentarily distracted by Margaret's shouting. They looked over, before continuing on to catch their trains. No one seemed inclined to take pity on the plight of the two unfortunates.

Philip looked around. The station was gradually emptying. A sad, grey light fell on the passers-by who all seemed to be anxious to get out of there. The ground was littered with the torn and trodden on pages of the free dailies. The ticket offices had long since closed. Philip was aware of a growing pressure on his throat, a feeling of having reached the end of the road with no going back. This station would be his terminus. The flash from a camera jerked him from his reverie. Ten little flashes popped one after the other before he understood what was going on. 'They're taking our picture,' he finally realised. 'The press are taking our picture!' He turned towards Margaret. She was giving the struggle everything she had, shrieking at the top of her lungs and offering to the cameras a face of martyrdom, grimacing, with tears of impotent rage and eyes raised heavenwards. Lalumière let go of Philip to chase after the young woman who had been snapping away for at least ten seconds. But she was too quick for him and scarpered, having taken a last shot of the gendarme as he ran at her. 'Damn it!' he exclaimed. Margaret beamed, sure of having made the front page. She graciously removed her hands from her pockets and offered them to be handcuffed.

Inspector Bouallem, arms flat on the desk, hands joined and head lowered, looked like a man concentrating. The walls of the small rectangular room were sparsely decorated with three photos of the city, a portrait of the president of the Republic, and a poster stating it was against the law to sell alcohol to minors. The window was slightly open, allowing in the damp, surprisingly chilly air. The inspector was daydreaming.

He was missing the midday sun of the Midi, and feeling nostalgic for the breakfasts at the Old Port of Marseilles he'd enjoyed as a sergeant stationed at Le Panier. The lowering Paris sky weighed on him like lead. Why was it so rarely blue? Since he had been transferred to Paris, having passed his exam three months previously, Samy had not had a moment to escape the confines of the city. He was suffocating. In his mind's eye he saw a schooner disappearing over the horizon, and unclasped his hands as if trying to capture the daydream that was already escaping him. The ringing of the telephone brought it to an abrupt end.

It was Sergeant Nguyen, talking loudly and quickly. Samy understood that something serious had happened at Gare du Nord. He couldn't quite grasp all the details. Two suspects had already been arrested and held. The platform was under surveillance. 'Incredible,' went on Nguyen, 'With all the security checks. Customs. Border police. Staff on the train.' Samy was beginning to lose patience. But Nguyen was still burbling excitedly, 'It was two of our military policemen who caught the suspects as they were trying to flee.'

The inspector cut him off. 'Just tell me what has happened!'

'A murder on the London to Paris express,' replied Nguyen.

'Are you sure? On a cross-Channel train?' clarified Bouallem.

'As sure as I am that it's you I'm talking to. I've seen the body.'

'I'm on the way. Keep hold of the suspects. Don't move. Don't do anything.' Bouallem was starting to feel excited himself.

A murder under the Channel! It was unbelievable. The cross-Channel train company were known for their tight security. They had increased their boarding security checks. The searches were careful, rigorous and effective. They were invasive, and passengers found them excessive. They were annoyed at having to undress every other time before being allowed on to the train. Overcoats, jackets, macs, shoes, belts, any kind of lace, watches, jewellery, scarves, trousers (if they were of a material thick enough to hide a knife, gun or explosives) and everything passengers were carrying, including little children's dolls and soft toys, went through the scanner. The company lived in permanent fear of a terrorist attack. If a bomb were to explode as the train was under the Channel, the tunnel would be exposed to the sea. Water would rush in on all sides with the speed of a tidal wave. A hole in the seabed and a shipwrecked train carried off into the maelstrom were the elements of the nightmare that haunted the train company engineers - along with the image of gigantic waves sent up by the explosion collapsing down on themselves in order to seal off brutally what would have become a giant underwater cemetery. This nightmare vision was the real reason why the security checks were so draconian at St Pancras and Gare du Nord. It was fear of the Flood.

Obviously the suspects were a pair of yobs. There must have been a brawl on the train. As he hurried off, the inspector tried to work out how such an inconceivable murder could have taken place. How could the train company have allowed two such obviously dangerous characters to get on the train? As he entered the station and crossed the concourse, Samy expected to find two beefy young blokes with shaved heads, their arms covered in tattoos, furious to have been handcuffed by the French police. When he spotted Nguyen, with the two military policemen flanking a little old couple, he immediately concluded that that imbecile of a sergeant had let the real culprits escape. 'Cretin!' he swore to himself.

'Hardly the moment to babysit the aged,' he threw at the soldiers, indicating Mr and Mrs Lewis. 'What are you playing at for God's sake?'

'Sir! These are the suspects,' Lalumière replied immediately, beaming, no doubt pleased to be able to get one over on this superior, whom he did not like the look of.

Samy turned to look at the two old people. Their hands were cuffed behind their backs and they were shuffling from foot to foot clearly at the drop from fatigue. They had been standing there, more or less at attention, for a good half hour, under the now indifferent eye of the rare passengers who crossed the concourse. The station would soon be closing. Two little Louis Vuitton suitcases lay at their feet, and they had been roughly opened, no doubt to search for the murder weapon.

It was crystal clear that these were not the murderers. Samy passed his hand through his hair. It was perhaps not a terrible blunder. The English couple might be important witnesses. But it was not good policing either. Under the withering gaze of the inspector, Lalumière began to realise his mistake. Margaret Lewis, who instinctively recognised the presence of a higher authority, pulled herself up in a dignified manner. She had calmed down, and her voice was more feeble now, but still firm: 'We are the victims here. It's a terrible injustice. We'll be filing a complaint. Count on it,' she declared to the inspector.

Samy apologised, and gave the order to release them. At the same time he advised the two officers to go off and see if they could find a drug-dealer to arrest, a pimp to fit up, or why not a prostitute while they were about it? 'What cave did you crawl out of?' he asked them without waiting for a response. They were as dissimilar from him as it was possible to be. The Arab remembered the way, as a child, he had been chased by soldiers through the little streets around the port of Aix. The two bozos in front of him believed the half-baked racism of populist discourse. They would have liked to rough him up. The anguished voice of Mrs Lewis reminding them of the injustice of their situation cut the altercation off before it could begin. The military policemen thought better of taking on Bouallem and scarpered instead.

'What shall we do with them?' Nguyen asked Samy, indicating the couple who hadn't moved since being released. 'Should we let them go?'

'Hang on, Nguyen. I think you've done enough already this evening.'

Samy pondered. What he had was two false suspects, perhaps two witnesses, but still no murder. The arrest of the English pair had taken precedence over solving the crime, as though nothing had happened on board the train. It was like a bad dream. Distraught, Samy looked over at the platforms where the cleaners were busy at work. Tomorrow the station would be as new. Then over on the left, right at the back of the concourse he spotted the platform reserved for the London train cordoned off with police tape. So it wasn't a dream. In his basic English, he explained to Margaret and Philip that they would be interrogated, because their testimony might be important. Margaret looked delighted. 'But you'll have to wait for an hour or so,' he added. Philip almost collapsed. The inspector wanted to visit the crime scene without more ado.

Two hours later Samy was back at the police station, his report in his pocket. A rather slight report. Apart from the mark on the victim's neck, the inspector had discovered nothing unusual. Everything in the first class carriage looked in order, that is to say, it looked extremely disorderly: beer cans, empty wine and champagne bottles, and miniatures of whisky, Ricard, gin and vodka were strewn on the floor along with greasy packaging and the crumbs from hastily devoured sandwiches. And of course the discarded newspapers and the books people had left behind in their haste to escape the train and sample the delights of the City of Light. Samy had left the station leaving the forensic team to collect fingerprints, saliva or hair if they could. It was unlikely that anything useful would be found. The crime was clearly the work of a professional.

The English couple, their hands no longer manacled, sat on a bench still waiting meekly. Although Margaret had put her head on her husband's shoulder and was snoring slightly, her chest rising and falling at regular intervals. Philip, wide-eyed, stared ahead of him. 'We'll be filing a complaint,' Samy recalled Margaret saying as he went over to them. The complaint was more embarrassing than the murder. It was after two in the morning. He would certainly be sanctioned if the photos Lalumière had mentioned appeared in the press, he told himself worriedly. He would be exiled to Saint-Pierre-et-Miquelon! That was the fate that awaited him. Supposing he just scarpered and went off on that schooner? He would sail off into the sunshine.

But Samy knew that that ship had sailed some time ago. You can't catch dreams. He looked at his watch again. Five past two. Desfeuillères had not replied to the message he had sent him at midnight. The lieutenant must have been having a great time at that hour. Samy still remembered the expression on his boss's face as he left the police station for the day. He'd said he had to go and buy something, and looked as if he relished the thought. Flowers for his wife, Samy had concluded. It was not the moment to disturb his boss.

Right. This English couple.

Samy made sure they were provided with water that they gulped down eagerly. 'Thank you, Captain.' That was what she called Samy. He inspired confidence in her. He was polite. She had noticed him straightaway as he came over to them at Gare du Nord. He was poised. She was trying to think why she had immediately felt at ease with the captain. When asked, Philip agreed he felt the same. The glass of water he had just offered them showed his worth.

'You see. He's a gentleman,' whispered Margaret.

As Samy took his seat behind his desk, she studied his figure, trim in the official uniform. The captain moved with elegance and grace, unlike the French, whom Mrs Lewis was beginning to abhor. She thought of the resort where she and her husband had spent their holidays. It had been on the island of Djerba in

Tunisia. A wonderful holiday. Beautiful island, blue sky, warm sea, and the resort staff had been charming. Unbelievable happiness, which had, alas, only lasted two weeks. They had then had to return to London, where it had rained for the whole of August. Along with the exotic food and the camel rides, Margaret had retained a glorious memory of Messaoud, the activity leader, who had been so wonderful at enlivening the long summer evenings with karaoke and fabulous dancing.

'Don't you think he looks like Messaoud?' she asked Philip, envisioning the sleek figure of the activity leader outlined against the blue of the Djerba sky.

Philip paused long enough to picture the captain minus his police uniform and dressed instead in a white djellaba: 'I see what you mean!'

Then they fell silent, gazing at Samy with a concentration that embarrassed him. Margaret was looking adoringly at him and Philip was frankly staring.

'I hope they're not nutty,' thought Samy worriedly.

Having given their address and full names etc, Philip and Margaret recounted their journey. They weren't fully in agreement and began to squabble about the reasons for their trip. They had come to Paris to relax, for pleasure, said Philip with heavy irony, for the sights, Margaret immediately corrected him. She wanted to see the Arc de Triomphe. She was just getting into her stride when Samy cut her off:

'Did you know the victim?'

'No we didn't!' they replied in unison.

Had they noticed him before they got on the train? No, because there were so many people at St Pancras. How would they notice an unknown face amid such a crowd? No, they hadn't noticed anything out of the ordinary either at St Pancras or on board the train, apart from the breakdown, of course. Samy was startled to learn there had been a breakdown. The train stopped right in the middle of the tunnel, Philip was explaining, when Margaret interrupted him to say, 'Not half way through, eighty per cent of the way, maybe.'

'You're wrong, Margaret. Completely wrong!' insisted Philip.

He had looked at his watch when the lights came back on. Samy was startled again. The damned English pair was drip-feeding him information. They were making fun of him. The train had been immobilised in the tunnel because of a power cut and they hadn't thought to mention that earlier? They were a wicked old pair. Samy was tempted to hold them as suspects. He raised his voice as he asked them why they hadn't told him earlier.

Margaret was immediately up in arms. She thought the captain's rebuke was very unfair. They hadn't thought that was worth mentioning because every passenger knew about it! Philip and she had nothing to add about the breakdown. That wasn't the reason they had been arrested, handcuffed even, and interrogated. But she added, dramatically, she would be happy to recount her entire life-story if that was what was required. Then she remembered the photographer who had taken a picture of their arrest. There would be an article in the *Sun* with pictures, and they would be interviewed. She would tell all. Philip, shrewder and more rational than his wife, was less enthusiastic. He explained that he and Margaret had seen nothing, noticed nothing, knew nothing. They could only tell him about their own journey. 'I wanted to see Paris,' he added as though confessing to a sin.

The interrogation had been going on for an hour. Samy was exhausted. He looked at Margaret and Philip. They looked tired, their complexions slightly red, and just like any other English couple come to Paris to drink late into the night without having to worry about the bell for last orders and eleven o'clock closing. The husband was right. They had nothing to declare. The best thing would be to dismiss them politely, having noted the address of their hotel. As Samy was thanking them with a forced smile, Margaret finally decided to put the question she had been burning to ask since the beginning of the interrogation:

'Captain! Are you from Djerba?'

Not immediately catching the meaning of the question, he asked for it to be repeated.

'Captain! Are you from Tunisia?'

Samy couldn't find a suitable answer. He had lost

patience with the couple. But Philip said, taking the captain's silence for agreement:

'We knew it.'

'Yes,' added Margaret, 'because you have such good manners.'

And she began to describe their trip to Djerba. She would have talked on until dawn had not the unexpected arrival of Lieutenant Desfeuillères in casual clothes forced her to save her happy account for later.

'Are you our taxi driver?' Philip asked, turning to Desfeuillères.

Roland Desfeuillères's first thought had been to make himself scarce. As soon as Juliette had closed the bedroom door, he had grabbed the car keys. There was nothing for him here. He had cast a last glance at the walls, the furniture, the red sofa and the egg-yolk-yellow armchairs, the books and other bits and pieces, and the few cheap, ugly knick-knacks. Everything was horrible. Roland no longer recognised himself in the interior from which his wife had just chased him, in a burst of anger, and for longer than she could possibly have imagined. Roland had closed the door quietly behind him like a thief stealing away without having taken anything. When he saw the two ridiculous little old people in their tourist clothes with their Louis Vuitton suitcases and their victim's arrogance, Roland felt the desire to flee again. What had he come to the police station for? Because there was nowhere else to go? Having downed three beers in three different bars, Roland had found himself on the street with no desire to go home. He had spent half an hour wandering around the central reservation of Boulevard de Clichy, disheartened by the trashy girls soliciting amongst the shadowy drug addicts. He had stopped the first taxi he saw on Place de Clichy, wondering what address he should give the driver. Perhaps he should just have continued on foot. For a moment the thought of exhausting himself by walking around until dawn was most appealing, but he was surprised to hear his voice shouting 'Taxi!' as he instinctively raised his arm. Now he was standing in his deputy's office looking at him and at two crazies who took him for a driver. His second thought was that it was time to take charge. He gave up any thought of fleeing.

Desfeuillères started talking to cut off his deputy's questions. He had been alarmed by the message Samy had sent at midnight. So he'd come immediately to see if he needed any help. That sounded simple and straightforward. But the lieutenant's friendly sentiments were belied by his crestfallen demeanour which he had not been able to disguise. His eyelids were swollen, his eyes empty and sad. In his neat little outfit reminiscent of a sailor, he looked like a partygoer who had been thrown out just as the party was heating up. Samy looked at his superior without saying anything. Why had he turned up? As if it wasn't enough that he had the English couple to deal with, now he was going to have to soothe his overwrought boss. The lieutenant stank of beer. But from what Samy knew of the lieutenant's planned evening, an amorous dinner with his wife in a restaurant, a bouquet of flowers and all the trappings, it shouldn't have been like that. Then Samy remembered that a corpse awaited him in the morgue. He would take his boss there, then buy him a coffee and send him home to his wife whether he wanted to go or not.

'We have a murder on our hands,' he said to him, without elaborating. 'And we have two witnesses who didn't see anything, and didn't hear anything either.'

Understanding that he was talking about them, Margaret and Philip looked up. 'It's not the driver,' whispered Margaret to her husband, listening to Desfeuillères talking to the man she no longer took for a captain. 'What if the other man is in charge?' she suddenly wondered in alarm.

A murder on a Friday evening was nothing much to write home about, thought Roland, listening to his deputy with half an ear. He was leaning against the wall, trying to make himself invisible. He would happily have disappeared inside the wall, if he could have. He was trying to think of a way of leaving unobtrusively. 'I could go to Deauville, I'd be there in the small hours to watch the sun rising over the Channel. Escape.' Suddenly his attention was caught by something his deputy was saying. The London to Paris express. 'What's he talking about?' wondered Desfeuillères who the moment before had been considering sailing across the Channel. Pushing himself away from the wall, he asked Samy what he had just said. What was going on?

Samy related the few facts that he had about the crime committed on board the train.

'Unbelievable!' exclaimed Desfeuillères, now standing up straight, his interest piqued.

He immediately demanded to read the deposition of the two witnesses that Nguyen had just printed off. Conscientiously, he had taken down every single detail. Captain this, Captain that, and finally the beauty salon at the Club Med in Djerba. Nguyen was laughing as he held out the two pages of testimony. Margaret and Philip did not find this reassuring. The unexpected arrival of the lieutenant made them nervous. His boorish manner and air of fatigue made them fear the worst. They were going to be locked up. 'And who knows for how long,' whispered Margaret to Philip, torn between delight and fear. At the very same moment the lieutenant whispered in his deputy's ear, 'Get these imbeciles out of here!'

Bouallem had very little information on the victim, other than his name, John Burny, and that he was a forty-five-year-old Glaswegian living in London. The Englishman, or rather the Scotsman, was travelling on his own, which, as Desfeuillères remarked to his assistant, did not help. He was unknown to the police, at least in France. Had he not been murdered, he would just have been any other tourist. But the murder had cast doubt on his apparent identity. Theft was not the motive for the crime. His designer sports bag, a wallet containing three thousand pounds and two credit cards had not been touched. And none of his papers had been stolen either. His passport was valid and appeared to be authentic. Perhaps it had been a settling of scores, but if so, both parties were well off, thought the lieutenant, becoming more and more intrigued. Perhaps Burny was an important figure in the underworld. But in that case wouldn't he already have been identified? The big-shots of the Mafia were all on record. At the same time the circumstances of his murder showed that the Scotsman couldn't just be an ordinary bloke. To stop a train under the Channel in order to commit a crime wasn't within the reach of just any criminal. Lost in conjecture, the lieutenant wondered whether Burny had been a spy. Had that been the case though, the Secret Service would already have made sure that the body and any traces of the murder had been removed. No trifling with the State, he thought to himself. Unfortunately the inadvertent reference to Musset's play reminded him of Juliette and his marriage. For the past three months *No Trifling with Love* had been lying around on his wife's desk. He liked the title and had taken to using 'trifling' whenever he could to Juliette's great pleasure. 'No trifling with the pasta cooking time, no trifling with money.' 'No trifling with policemen,' replied Juliette. That had been four or five months ago. An eternity. And suddenly Roland realised that he and Juliette would probably divorce. His next thought was of John Burny. The lieutenant wanted to see the body. 'Now?' Bouallem asked him, surprised. He was dead on his feet, and had decided to leave viewing the body until the next day. His only desire was to get rid of his boss and quietly finish out his night shift. But Desfeuillères was adamant – he wanted to view Burny's body, he was curious to see what he looked like. He needed to see that body. As Desfeuillères had listened to his deputy, he had had the feeling they were dealing with a ghost. Burny didn't exist. Curiously, Roland found it hard to believe what his deputy was telling him. 'Aren't you going home to go to bed?' Bouallem finally asked him. 'Now!' exclaimed Desfeuillères. 'We're not going to let him get away.' The lieutenant seemed to be agitated. Samy looked at him in alarm. It was three o'clock in the morning. His boss was out of his mind.

On the contrary, Roland felt as if he were finally fully focused. He had not been so engaged by a murder for a long time, too long, probably. He suddenly felt that curiosity he had experienced as a child that had driven him to become a policeman. He liked mysteries. A crime was just a series of questions. How? Why? Who? Questions you had to keep repeating like a child who is never satisfied with the answers he's given. 'Papa, why does the sun orbit the earth? Why is there only one sun? And why does the world exist?' Burny was a bit like the universe. You couldn't see where he came from or where he was going. And you could tell even less who he actually was.

The station had long since been closed and the metal grilles would be padlocked. The train was still at the platform, and would be inaccessible until morning, Bouallem explained. The body had been removed and taken to the morgue. There was nothing to see. Desfeuillères then reproached his deputy for not calling him. 'I would have come immediately,' he told him, thinking that the phone call would have spared him an evening he could well have done without. But the evening was obviously not over yet, and Burny had conveniently turned up to distract the lieutenant. Bouallem relented.

Desfeuillères's passion for leading investigations had lessened as he sank into a married life whose only tangible result was the gradual extinction of any kind of desire. His appetite for mysteries waned at the same pace as his libido, he thought as he absent-mindedly watched the deserted streets of Paris flash pass the windows of the car that was taking him and his deputy to the morgue of the Pitié-Salpêtrière hospital. At Place de l'Opéra, he realised that his last criminal success had been down merely to his professionalism. Bouallem drove in silence, having received no reply to his banal comment on the chill of the night. As he watched the Colonne de Juillet heaving into view, Roland concluded that he had let himself become imprisoned by routine. He saw how that happened after so many years in the Criminal Investigation Department. But in fact the same thing had happened with Juliette. From force of habit he had learned how to please Juliette, but they were both bored. He was despairing as he realised that their sexual satisfaction was just the result of well-intentioned hard work. And that was how Roland had succeeded in his career, even though his ambition had long since been blunted. He watched the Seine flowing as they drove over the Pont d'Austerlitz. For several years, a vague, diffuse unhappiness had slowed him down, progressively thickening his features and his figure, and reducing his smile, once so incisive and mocking, to nothing more than a relaxing of his mouth. Physically as well as mentally, Desfeuillères thought he had become unappealing, although fortunately other people still seemed to find him sympathetic. He was a friendly guy, serious, a good father, a good husband, overall thoroughly likeable. Yet he was heading for meltdown. By the time they had reached Boulevard de l'Hôpital, he had surprised himself by counting how many years before he could retire. That led inexorably to thinking how many years until his death which would he thought probably be at about seventy, although why he should think he would live less than the national average was not clear to him. When Samy parked the car outside the hospital, Roland understood that he was already in meltdown. 'I'm at the end of my rope,' he thought as he slowly extricated himself from the car.

'Is there a problem, Lieutenant?' Samy asked him.

The doctor uncovered John Burny's naked body, as the lieutenant looked impatiently on. Then he exclaimed:

'He's in great shape! How old did you say he was?'

'Forty-five.'

The victim looked younger than Desfeuillères, although he was five years older. In spite of himself Desfeuillères felt envious, jealous even, hardly an appropriate reaction to the sight of the unfortunate man. The body was stiff. 'He was already cold when I discovered him in his seat,' Bouallem told his boss, whose concentration on the victim he was finding disturbing. The lieutenant seemed to be fascinated. The state of the body had been noted in the statement. 'Rigor mortis,' Samy had written. It was now one thirty in the morning. From which it was possible to calculate the approximate time of death, confirming the hypothesis that the death had occurred as the train was in the tunnel under the Channel. The train had left London at 20.05. At 20.39, it entered the tunnel and would have emerged twenty minutes later, had it not broken down for ten minutes. So the train had entered French soil at 21.09, or 22.09, French time. Rigor mortis only sets in three hours after death. The muscles stiffen and the body turns to marble as if death sculpts its own tomb. John Burny was alive when the train entered the tunnel, he was dead when it emerged, and rock hard by the time Samy had examined the body. 'This murder could not just be random, the breakdown of the train was no accident,' reflected the lieutenant out loud.

'Shall we go?' asked Samy, as the doctor was preparing to push the body back into its cold chamber.

'No way. I haven't seen anything yet,' replied Desfeuillères, then asked the doctor for a pair of surgical gloves.

'What else is there to see?' Samy was growing impatient. The morgue was making him feel nauseous, and his boss was making him uneasy.

'What is it you're hoping to find?' he asked, raising his voice. 'He's not going to start speaking to us.'

'You never know,' the lieutenant immediately replied, excitedly.

'I'll leave you to it,' the doctor then declared, throwing Samy a sympathetic glance. 'I'm going to get some coffee.'

Left alone with his boss, Samy wondered how on earth the lieutenant had spent the evening that it had left him in such a state. He had never seen him so hyped up. Crazy! His boss had become crazy. But Desfeuillères had already pulled on the gloves and was beginning to palpate the body.

'So!' he finally said to his deputy. 'Burny is or rather

was a regular gym goer. Look at his muscle definition. I would be prepared to bet, taking account of his age, that he works out twice a week. So he was someone who took good care of himself. His haircut is immaculate. Probably cut this week.' Then lowering his voice. 'His pubic hair has recently been waxed, yesterday or the day before. For religious reasons? Or more likely because he's single and looking for action. He's not wearing a ring. Not a blemish from head to toe. No scars, not a mark anywhere, apart from the strangulation mark round his neck.' The murderer had used a lace or rather a very resistant nylon string. The back of the neck was all purple. And the mark was clear. The murderer had known what he was doing. He had succeeded first time. Obviously an expert. The Scotsman would have suffered very little. He wouldn't have had time to realise what was happening to him before expiring.

The lieutenant raised his head to look inquiringly at his deputy. Something was bothering him. He couldn't make out what was wrong with the murder, but it was too neat and tidy to be believable. Samy was speechless, impressed by his boss's fascination with the dead man. 'You're right,' he said finally. 'You wouldn't take him for a victim.'

'Exactly!' exclaimed Desfeuillères, putting his gloved hand on his deputy's shoulder. Samy instinctively took a step back. 'What's wrong is that the Scot clearly did not anticipate his untimely end. He doesn't look like someone on his guard. And if he were, why wax the night before? So he was murdered by a man or a woman who had something against him without him realising. The fact that he was unaware isn't going to help us solve the crime. Let's turn him over to see if he's hiding something.'

The doctor returned just as Desfeuillères and Bouallem were taking hold of the body.

'Am I interrupting something?' inquired the doctor, a touch sarcastically.

'You might give us a hand!' replied Samy.

'Fine pair of buttocks,' Desfeuillères then commented, laughing.

The other two looked at him in astonishment. But he went on, as if talking to himself, 'As well as working out twice a week, he must go running regularly. I bet he runs every Sunday for an hour. With short strides, I should think.'

Day was breaking by the time the two policemen got back into the car. Bouallem took the wheel with the idea of dropping Desfeuillères at home. He would do it without asking the lieutenant. In the dingy early morning light his boss looked even more drawn, and his hair wild and greasy. Samy had the uncomfortable feeling of sitting beside a stranger. He was driving down the deserted Boulevard de l'Hôpital when a young woman suddenly crossed the road. She had appeared out of the blue, like an apparition and was walking slowly, indifferent to the world around her. Samy stopped the car just in time. She must have been no more than sixteen or seventeen. Light-footed. Her ballet pumps seemed barely to touch the ground. She suddenly turned her head towards their car and gave Samy a wide smile, full of *joie de vivre*. The next moment she disappeared, hurrying off as though she had just become aware of the danger. 'On the way to school?' wondered Samy. But it was much too early to be going to school. Samy then wondered what he could have deduced from the girl's body had fate landed her on the mortuary slab. Could he have divined the vitality that she exhibited with such confidence? She must have stayed out all night. Bouallem would have staked his life on it. Her smile had been for the young lover whose arms she had just left. Only happiness could have accounted for her self-satisfaction.

Desfeuillères pulled him from his reverie. 'We did actually learn something from the Scotsman,' he said. 'We learned the reason for his trip to Paris.' Samy gave a start, jerking the steering wheel so much they almost crashed into a tree.

'Watch out! You'll get us killed as well!'

An hour earlier as Desfeuillères had been thinking about the victim, death had seemed rather appealing. Now, on the contrary, he felt a desire to live so strong he found it hard to explain. After reprimanding his deputy, he continued with what he had been saying, without giving Samy the chance to respond.

'The Scot was coming to Paris for a good time. He probably had a date. A demanding mistress. Why bother to wax otherwise? The more I think about it, the more obvious Burny's journey seems. The only hitch is that he never made it into the arms of his mistress. The murder looks like a mistake. The Scotsman was in the wrong place at the wrong time. And yet he was strangled by a professional, a man who didn't get it wrong, and never failed in his mission. It promises to be an exciting investigation,' he said in conclusion, watching the sun rise over the towers of Notre-Dame.

Samy had not been listening to Desfeuillères.

'Shall I take you home?' he asked him as they drove into Place de la Bastille.

'Home?' replied the lieutenant in amazement. 'Take me to the police station – now.'

Desfeuillères turned his computer on before he had even sat down properly at his desk. As the machine was slowly warming up, he sent a text message to Juliette. 'Don't wait for me.' Short but to the point. Roland had nothing else to add. Like a snake sloughing off his skin, Desfeuillères had just shed his former existence without a backwards glance and with no remorse or regret. He typed John Burny onto his glittering screen and hit 'search.'

4

The train had passed Lille and was rapidly approaching the coast. Lieutenant Desfeuillères watched the time tick by on his watch: 18.15. Ten minutes from now the express train would plunge under the Channel. The investigation would begin in the darkness of the tunnel. 'In ten minutes, who knows?' thought Roland. 'Maybe I'll find a lead.'

The lieutenant had insisted on travelling first class, in spite of the additional cost. He wanted to reconstruct the journey that had carried John to his death, in the same conditions if in the other direction; Roland would begin in Paris and end in London. He had made sure he was allocated the same seat as John, towards the rear of the carriage on the left-hand side. There was just one seat behind him, so he had a good view of almost everyone else in the carriage. John had found himself in a fortunate position. From here he could see without being seen, with the exception of that one row behind. That was where the crime had been committed. The first or last row, depending on the direction of travel, must have been occupied by the murderer, long enough to carry out the killing at least. When Roland sat down in his single seat, the one behind him was empty and he hoped it would remain so in a macabre echo of the fateful journey. But shortly after the train set off, a man in his forties came to sit behind him. A banker, judging by his reading material, he had promptly unfolded his newspaper and was yet to put it down. Roland grumbled to himself at this last-minute arrival. The man had not got up once. Buried in his copy of the *Financial Times*, he didn't notice Desfeuillères's frequent glances in the direction of the seat he had, as far as Roland was concerned, stolen. The lieutenant was trying to understand or rather to visualise how the murderer had gone about the attack. It had been clean, precise, executed to perfection. How had the killer managed to strangle the person in front of him without alerting the entire carriage?

18.20. The transit through the tunnel would begin in less than five minutes. Roland looked outside. Heavy rain was pounding against the windows. The wind was blowing from the east, whipping the side of the train. Inside the carriage, several of the passengers had drifted off, oblivious to the raging storm. Leaning his head against the window, the lieutenant was daydreaming. In the ten days since the launch of the investigation he had insisted on running, his whole world had been turned upside down. Today he was not only leaving Paris, but the life he had lived up until now. It had not been difficult to say goodbye to Juliette: 'I'm leaving,' and that was it, more or less. Swiftly thereafter, with a haste that left his wife stunned, he had moved on to the matter of the children, the apartment and finally the divorce proceedings, which met with no resistance.

The rain suddenly got much heavier, falling in deafening torrents. Distracted from his thoughts by the din, Roland looked up. The northern plains had disappeared from sight, as though drowned under the deluge. The Channel already? The dull rattling of the rain brought back the memory of a summer's night. A storm had erupted while he and Juliette were on holiday for a fortnight in a small hotel room on the shores of Lake Annecy. Frightened by the lightning, she had run into Roland's arms. He had whispered a few words of reassurance and held her tightly. After a while, he had gradually begun caressing her breasts, which were lit every so often by flashes of lightning. Why had he left her? The rain suddenly stopped. The train fell silent. It was already dark. The picture of Juliette vanished from his mind, driven out by the shadows. The train had just gone under the Channel.

The morning after the murder, the lieutenant had started off at the station, looking for information on the victim and finding none. John Burny's name did not appear in any international police files. Afterwards

Roland headed to Gare du Nord to meet the border police. The victim was unknown to them too. His next step was to contact the British authorities. They had nothing on Burny either. There had been some debate over which of the two national forces ought to take charge of the investigation. It was eventually decided that the case fell under French jurisdiction, the murder having apparently been committed on French soil. Desfeuillères remained unconvinced. There was no way of knowing in exactly which part of the tunnel the murder had taken place. What was certain, on the other hand, was that the British wanted nothing to do with it. Whether it was laziness, or national pride, or some other secret reason, Roland wasn't about to wait for them to change their minds. He wanted this investigation and the British were more than happy to give it to him – too happy, it seemed to him. He still had to convince the public prosecutor to hand him the reins. A lunch in Place des Vosges saw to that. Later, Roland returned to the hotel room he had booked himself into that morning and called Juliette.

'I'm checking into a hotel for a few days. We both need space to think things through.' Roland chose his words carefully. 'We can do that more easily on our own. I'll call you on Tuesday or Wednesday.'

At the other end of the line, his wife had initially sounded surprised. 'I didn't think it was as bad as that. You were just a bit thoughtless.' Roland said nothing.

'OK, whatever you want.' Juliette fully expected her cop to turn up on her doorstep the next morning.

The train was speeding along in the darkness. Roland felt a kind of childish excitement at being under the Channel. Perhaps they would be able to look out at the fish through the windows, transformed into portholes for the occasion. But what if the whole thing caved in? The prevailing calm of the carriage quickly allayed his fears. The tunnel was solid.

The investigation began here. The killer must have taken advantage of the power outage to sneak into John's carriage. That was the logical conclusion. Roland found it hard to imagine a murderer sitting quietly behind his victim for the entire length of the journey. Burny would have spotted him, sensed danger. But that was supposing the victim knew what was coming, that Burny was on the defensive. There was nothing to support such a hypothesis. On the contrary, the smile Desfeuillères believed he had seen playing on John's cold features suggested he hadn't suspected a thing. Even in death, he looked a picture of happiness. In fact, this was what had struck the lieutenant the most on his visit to the morgue. Burny was so fit and healthy-looking for a dead man! In any case, it was certain the murderer had acted while the train was at a standstill; whether or not he had been sitting there since the start of the journey did not change much. The murderer knew that the train would break down and the power would fail, that was the crux of it. And to know such a thing meant having the means to organise it and the necessary contacts on the inside. A man doesn't stop a train on his own. The killer had to know someone, or several people, on the staff of the train company. Having got that straight, the rest was a matter of deduction. He would: 1) find out how you go about stopping a train travelling at high speed (and beneath the sea at that); 2) question the management about their employees (when was the mechanic taken on?); 3) speak to the driver of the train: ask for his thoughts on the breakdown – did such things happen regularly, rarely, almost never? 4) ascertain whether the killer was still on board the train when it arrived at Gare du Nord, or had fled once his job was done (get hold of a map of the tunnel: look at fire escape routes). It was shaping up to be a long and complex investigation. This realisation cheered the lieutenant's spirits. It meant there would be no rush to get back to Paris.

The train suddenly slowed right down. The lights flickered briefly. 'I must be dreaming,' thought Desfeuillères, pinching himself. He turned round. Behind him, the man with the *Financial Times* was fast asleep with his mouth wide open. His newspaper was unfurled at his feet. By clambering up on his seat and peering over, Roland was able to read the page the man had got to before going to sleep. It was filled with columns of figures and percentages. The stock market was continuing to fall. The previous day, Roland had heard about several businesses on the brink of liquidation. The banks had stopped lending. Was the sleeping man a ruined banker, one of the traders splashed over the front pages for the last ten days? He might have been dead, but for the thin stream of air coming out of his mouth. Could John Burny have been secretly working on behalf of one of the big banks? Perhaps disgruntled shareholders had ordered his death. The lieutenant sank back into his seat and glanced out of the window. The train was enveloped by pitch darkness; it was impossible even to make out the roof of the tunnel. There were no windows looking out onto the sea or paper lanterns to light their route. They were lost in the middle of nowhere, cut off from everything and everyone. 'And with no way of making a call', thought Roland as he looked at his phone, which had no service. A tunnel under the sea was the ideal place to commit murder. The hit had been well planned and thought through. The only sound was the regular thumping of the wheels against the rails, a dull, monotonous thud that made you want to go to sleep. Indeed, everyone in the carriage seemed to be dozing. All conversation had ceased and the laughter had dried up. A strange calm reigned, as if the life had slowly drained out of the carriage, and probably the entire train. Where was this high-speed engine taking them, beneath the sands of the English Channel?

Towards which tomb were they headed? Juliette's face appeared before the lieutenant's anxious eyes as a final reminder of the life he was leaving behind. He recalled a line from a French poem his wife had recited to him some three weeks earlier: *Dans la nuit du tombeau, toi qui m'as consolé*. Roland was trying to remember how it went on and to put his finger on the name of the poet, when a tall blond man walking down the aisle brought him back to reality with a literal thud. The guy didn't look much over twenty and, with his above-average height and gangly arms, he appeared encumbered by his own body. He walked clumsily, knocking into heads that protruded into the aisle, unintentionally waking passengers as he went. The headphones wedged inside both ears made him deaf to the chaos he left in his wake. As he passed Roland, he almost fell against his shoulder; he was probably drunk, too.

Who was John Burny? The information the lieutenant had gathered about him before his departure remained thin – not much more than a name, when all was said and done. The police officer in London he had managed to get on the phone had not been very helpful, merely confirming the details printed on John's passport. Male. White British. Member of the Presbyterian Church. Born in Glasgow on 16 August 1963. Single. A second call had given Desfeuillères a bit more to go on. John Burny was an estate agent. He worked for a small independent company based in Pimlico. Having moved to London at the age of twenty, Burny appeared to have lived a life without incident. He was not known to the police. At the end of the call, the officer had given Roland the address and telephone number of the estate agency, which was just around the corner from the victim's home address.

The lieutenant had arranged to meet his British counterpart two days after his arrival. He had not found it too difficult to understand him, in spite of or perhaps because of the strong accent that made him pronounce his 'r's in the rasping French way. He did, however, have trouble catching the man's name. At first he had heard it as Satadji, then Seutadji, before finally wondering if it wasn't simply Sir Sadji. He had a little under forty-eight hours to work it out. He could look him up, to find out for certain. If the Englishman had been less than forthcoming on the phone, Roland had in turn lied about the date of his arrival, claiming to be getting to London at ten o'clock on the Wednesday morning. Convention had it that the first thing a police officer did upon landing on foreign soil was to touch base with the local force, who would look after him, show him around, and to all intents and purposes manipulate him. Roland preferred to arrive on the Monday to give himself a chance to work out the victim's lifestyle on his own. His counterpart's coolness and lack of curiosity about the case had reassured the lieutenant as to his intentions. The man did not seem very inclined to help him. Desfeuillères got the impression that the case presented no more interest to him than a common road accident. This air of boredom and reluctance to go into detail had surprised Roland at first. As soon as he put the phone down, however, his surprise began to turn to suspicion. The Brits were hiding something. Soon Roland had developed a fully fledged theory. John Burny had been travelling under a false identity. That meant this was a sensitive situation. State secrets might be at stake, a conspiracy between banks or an arms deal, perhaps. Then, feeling suddenly overwhelmed by the potential scope of the investigation awaiting him in London, Roland asked himself if in fact the whole thing couldn't just have been an accident. John's name was indeed Burny. A crazy person had randomly killed him and then been lost in the crowd of disembarking passengers at Gare du Nord. 'But that doesn't mean I'm ready to close my case,' concluded the lieutenant as the train emerged from the tunnel.

The sun was out. A warm late summer light shone over the English countryside. The big, reddening sun was going down, slowly dwindling over the horizon. Its golden rays looked cheaply gilded. As autumn moved in, the star was selling off its former glories. Yet it still had its pride and managed to pull the wool over the eyes of the world. As soon as they were outside the tunnel, the passengers turned in unison to look at the light, dazzling their eyes which had become accustomed to darkness. Conversations resumed and laughter rang out heartily once more. Droves of people left their seats to head for the buffet carriage. They could breathe again. Roland watched the cars on a road running alongside the railway tracks. They were driving on the left. This was England alright. He was reminded of a trip to Brighton he had made aged seventeen.

'The happy isle!' he exclaimed.

The following morning Roland was scouring the properties for sale in the window of Dreams of Chelsea estate agents. A studio flat was on the market for £300,000 while a large two-bed ('incredibly spacious – must be seen', according to the advert) had an asking price of two million. There were a few places for rent, relegated to the bottom of the display. A nice-looking one-bed near Victoria station was going for £600 a week. Far beyond the means of the lieutenant. Dreams of Chelsea lived up to its name. Nothing on its books was within reach of the average Joe. The young woman sitting inside with her eyes glued to her computer screen was no doubt equally inaccessible.

After checking his watch, the lieutenant made up his mind to go inside. He had made an appointment for eleven o'clock. The young woman looked up with a smile.

'May I help you?'

The lieutenant explained who he was. The woman's face dropped.

'I'd forgotten you were coming,' she said by way of welcome.

Desfeuillères looked away, unsure what to say. The economic crisis was making itself felt here. Of the three desks, only one was occupied. The office was too neat and tidy. It was obvious that no clients had walked through the door since opening time. The woman's smile had been too eager. She was desperate for business. Having recovered from her misunderstanding, she introduced herself.

'Kate Reed. What can I do for you?'

Her tone had softened and the look on her face now expressed interest, if not much warmth. She was eyeing the lieutenant closely.

'Tell me about John Burny,' he said.

Miss Reed began by expressing her disbelief. She was stunned by the news. 'How could this happen? John was so full of life!'

People always reacted in the same way to the death of a loved one, stubbornly and stupidly refusing to accept what had happened. The deceased had been alive the last time they saw them. No shit. They couldn't understand how somebody could give them the slip, just like that. If it wasn't for the tragedy of the situation, they would consider the dead person's behaviour really rather rude. Death never did possess manners. Eventually, having expressed her dismay in every way she could, Kate confessed she really didn't have much to say about John.

'He was charming, a very thoughtful person. John was a good guy. Who could have wanted him dead?'

Roland was only half listening. Kate had stood up in order to carry on the conversation at closer proximity. She had positioned herself in front of Roland, leaning back against her desk at an angle that showed off her body to its advantage. She wanted to be looked at. Roland obliged. Wearing a thin, close-fitting jumper and skinny jeans, Kate Reed dressed to please. She was smiling again, but it was a different kind of smile from the over-keen one she had given Roland on mistaking him for a client. This was a smile that meant to be friendly and open yet remained slightly guarded, as though holding something back. There was no denying Kate was a sexy woman. The way she perched on the edge of her desk spelled it out, if it was ever in doubt. As far as John Burny was concerned, she was remarkably composed. Even her sadness was sleek.

'You're not giving me much to go on,' Roland eventually interrupted her. 'Are you telling me he never had the slightest problem with anybody? No skeletons in the closet whatsoever?'

'That's not what I said,' replied Kate, slightly shifting her position to better display her shoulders, which her light cotton jumper had dropped to reveal slightly.

'John wasn't a straightforward character. Of course he had his fair share of problems. But he didn't talk about them – not often, anyway.'

Roland couldn't decide whether to be annoyed or amused by her.

'Go ahead, tell me about them.'

Kate continued to look at him closely. Something about the lieutenant had caught her eye and she wasn't afraid to admit it. The fact he was French was nothing to write home about; his compatriots were in and out of her office all the time. But a French cop, *un flic*, as she had been repeating to herself since leaving her desk, now *that* was a much rarer commodity.

'I don't see how I can sum John up in just a few words. There's so much to say.' She was smiling unabashedly as she spoke. 'How can I describe him? He's just John. I mean, he was John. I can't get my head around the fact he's gone. It was so unexpected.'

Having abruptly decided he had heard enough, Roland was beginning to gather his things when, as if propelled by invisible springs, Kate practically pounced on him.

'Shall we go and talk about John somewhere more comfortable?'

'What time?' the lieutenant shot back with a level of self-assurance that surprised even himself.

'Seven o'clock. Come and pick me up from here. Do you like Thai food?'

'The happy isle,' Roland said to himself again as he left the estate agency. The encounter had lasted no more than ten minutes. It had been brief but promising. The lieutenant was none the wiser about John, aside from the fact he was a charming guy. 'No wonder', thought Roland, 'who wouldn't be nice to Kate?' He was already itching to see her again to find out more about her. It was seven hours until the time they had arranged to meet. Seven hours of freedom or seven hours to kill. It all came down to how he chose to spend the day. London was as much of a mystery to him as John was. He had intended to begin his investigation by looking into the life of the victim. Instead, he would start with the city itself. But which angle should he focus on? Where should he begin? he wondered, looking this way and that, all of a sudden feeling lost. He could unfold the map he had bought the previous day at St Pancras, but all maps did was lay out the position of the streets; they didn't give you reasons to visit anywhere. In a single glance, your eye could sweep over so many places you would never actually see. Open the guidebook he had bought at Gare du Nord? He didn't feel like following the tourist trail. Walking around blindly seemed the safest option. Roland took the first road on the right.

It was a quaint little area. Handsome white three-storey townhouses gave the neighbourhood the feeling of a sleepy seaside resort in low season. Roland wandered past the shop windows, an Italian deli here, a wine merchant there and a cheesemonger further on. He was taking time to soak it all in. This was John's neck of the woods. Roland turned right and then left, wiggling between streets, trying to work out possible routes between the estate agency and the victim's home. That was where his feet were leading him: Moreton Place. The previous night, in his hotel room on Belgrave Road, he had looked at a map of the area, known as Pimlico. He had initially been surprised at the Italian-sounding name. *Piazza del Popolo* ... *Pimlico*. Now he realised the area didn't feel Italian in the slightest. The bijou abodes of Pimlico, with their sash windows and columns either side of the door, looked more like doll's houses than transalpine palaces. Bordered by the Thames to the south and Victoria station and the railway to the west, the area had a village feel. There were few pedestrians on its quiet streets and even fewer cars, all of them driving slowly. Pimlico seemed a world away from the hustle and bustle of the city which Roland had tasted on his arrival at St Pancras the previous day. The impression left by Pimlico on the passer-by was one of a haven of peace, a pleasant place to while away a few days. 'Start a new life?' wondered Roland, stopping outside an antiques dealer. In the window, the wide gilt-framed mirrors returned his reflection. On what whim had John Burny taken that train to Paris? Everything was expensive. Roland walked on.

Having reached Moreton Place, he had no trouble locating John Burny's address at number 14. It was a modestly sized white house that looked exactly like all the other houses around Moreton Place, a clean and tidy lane with baskets of geraniums hanging from the streetlights on either side. John lived on the ground floor. In his absence, the curtains remained closed. Roland was pausing to admire the facade of the building when an eccentrically dressed old lady with green hair appeared out of nowhere, giving him a start.

'There's no use hanging around out here,' she told him. 'John's not at home. He's gone off God knows where, and he didn't even come and say goodbye. The swine!' she cackled, revealing a sorry set of teeth. And with that she was on her way again, without waiting for a response.

The lieutenant took a notebook out of his jacket pocket and scrawled: 'J. B. well known to his neighbours. Seems well liked.' It was rather a meaningless comment and merely echoed what Kate Reed had said. John had been a charming kind of guy. The lieutenant was getting pretty sick of hearing that word.

There was a coffee shop on the corner; might John have been a regular? The waitress to whom Roland put this question before she even handed him his espresso confirmed that indeed he was. She had worked here for over a year and knew John well. Or rather, had known him, she corrected herself. Word of his death had spread around the area as early as Monday morning. People had learned the news on picking up their copies of the *Daily Mirror*. The cover was taken up with an image of an English couple who had been mistreated at the hands of the French police. The paper's commentary was scathing: a scandal, a disgrace. 'The End of the *Entente Cordiale*?' asked the headline. The reporting of the murder itself ('Brit killed in unprovoked attack') was left to the footnotes. The news had come as a shock. John had got on with everyone. The waitress seemed to have got on with him even better than most. She couldn't find enough words to sing his praises. Friendly, considerate ('He always had a kind word for me when I brought him his coffee'), stylish, well-dressed, basically a charming kind of guy. She couldn't believe he was dead. A group of tourists entered the cafe, forcing her to break off her account. It was obvious she was torn up about the murder. She could have gone on talking about John for an hour. Roland took advantage of the fortuitous interruption to pay for his coffee and slip out of the cafe, writing in his notebook: 'Known by everyone, well liked, a charmer.' Who could possibly hold anything against him? A woman scorned? No, that was ridiculous: love didn't stop trains.

Walking back towards Victoria, the lieutenant came across a gym. He remembered John's impressive muscle tone; even lying on the slab, he still looked good. The bastard! The waitress at the cafe, an attractive girl of about twenty with a fit body, had barely looked at Roland but had not been immune to the charms of the Scotsman, despite the fact the man was five years his senior. Thank goodness for Kate, who had looked

Roland up and down and liked what she'd seen. He totted up the hours that still lay between him and their date. The day did not seem to be moving forward. Roland pushed open the door to the gym. This must be where John came to work out.

At reception, a tall, sour-faced redhead handed him a membership form before he had a chance to say a word. The price varied according to your choice of activities. It was expensive, whichever package you opted for. This obviously didn't bother Burny. Roland soon realised he wouldn't get anything out of the dragon who had clearly been put there to scare off riff-raff. This wasn't a gym for just anybody. The lieutenant filled in an information sheet, giving his address as the estate agent's. Under 'Activities' he ticked 'muscle toning'. When he handed over his credit card, the redhead immediately lightened up, struggling to suppress a giggle of satisfaction.

'Welcome!'

The gym operated flexible hours. The fitness suite closed at 10 p.m. 'Tomorrow', Roland told himself, 'I'll start tomorrow. I'm bound to meet a few of John's old mates while I'm here. And an hour's exercise won't do me any harm either.' The lieutenant had never joined a gym before. 'Good old John,' he couldn't help saying to himself as he left the building.

Ten minutes later Roland was standing outside Victoria station. He was hungry. He looked at his watch. One o'clock. A dozen double-decker buses were fighting for space, coming and going, constantly on the move. The city was abuzz. The mouth of the Tube spat out regular bursts of several hundred commuters, who immediately scattered onto the station concourse or into the surrounding streets. People were hailing taxis, newspaper vendors pressed their ill tidings on passing punters, a sandwich-board man was advertising a trattoria less than two hundred yards away. Roland found himself getting caught up in the excitement of the capital. Pimlico was now nothing more than a memory, belonging to another time.

The lieutenant let himself be swept along with a crowd of people boarding a bus. As soon as the doors closed, the driver – a wide load in himself – set the bus lurching into motion, causing all those clinging to the handrails to sway in unison. Roland was hoping to get to the top deck to enjoy a view over the city, but instead found himself squashed up against a stout woman chewing the fat with another two old bags. They stood right in the middle of the aisle in everyone's way, as impervious to their fellow passengers as to the movement of the bus. Every time the bus stopped, Roland bent down to try to see where they were. Westminster Cathedral. Parliament. The bus was heading into central London. Whitehall. The three friends finally piped down. Trafalgar Square. There was a mass exodus of people descending from the bus in droves. Roland seized the opportunity to take a seat next to the window as dozens of new passengers began to board. Nelson's Column. The National Gallery. He could still get off here before the doors closed. Without knowing quite why, the lieutenant told himself the National Gallery wasn't the kind of place where Burny would have spent his time. Besides, he hadn't come to London to admire the works of the Old Masters. Squeezed against the window, he felt a new sense of trepidation at the task that lay ahead. With every step he took, John Burny seemed to slip further from his grasp. A charming guy! That was the only thing he had so far managed to learn about the man. An anonymous tide of pedestrians moved slowly and inexorably up and down the wide pavements of Haymarket. Strings of gaudy shop signs passed before the lieutenant's eyes, but he barely saw them. Where might John have gone when he wanted to get out of Pimlico? The bus had just come to a stop. Piccadilly Circus. 'I'm getting off!'

Tourists swarmed around the famous fountain taking pictures that served as their own personal postcards. The lieutenant was already regretting getting off at this stop. There was no way John would have hung out around here. Roland's painfully rumbling stomach had been the motive for his sudden exit from the bus. Standing back at a slight remove, a sandwich-board man pointed to a sushi place a hundred yards away. A few moments later, Roland was sitting at a table in an empty restaurant, quickly scanning the menu which had been brought to him by a waitress who looked more Chinese than Japanese, in his opinion. Half an hour later, with a selection of ten pieces of sushi, sashimi and skewers in his stomach, he was back treading the pavements of Piccadilly. But where was he aiming for? This tour was not going to plan. Roland was trying to get a picture of the city as a whole, but was getting bogged down in the details. The city, like the victim, was slipping through his fingers. A smartly dressed young woman cut ahead of him. He fell into step behind her. She was heading towards Green Park.

Having admired the window displays at Fortnum & Mason, Caviar House and the Ritz, Roland arrived in the gallery district. Art galleries had grown around Piccadilly like buds in springtime, drawn by the heat of the cash being spent on every corner. The usual old-fashioned stuff – the Watteaus, Goyas and Gainsboroughs – was hung side-by-side with the most cutting-edge, off-the-wall creations, like the shark immortalised in a tank of formaldehyde. Roland trailed from one exhibit to the next, casting cursory glances through the glass. This world was foreign to him. There was art in the way the galleries were laid out and decorated, too; they were always thoughtfully designed and decked out with prime materials like marble, steel or even gold. In one of the rooms, there was a skull and crossbones on which the artist had painted a chessboard. By association of ideas, Roland thought he saw John smiling back at him. John hadn't quite lost the match against death. The lieutenant's investigation was keeping him alive. Roland owed it to him to keep going. After all, wasn't it thanks to John that he had been able to drop everything all in one go, the apartment, his wife and even his kids? If it wasn't for John, he wouldn't be strolling round the choicest parts of London right now. John must have been the kind of guy who liked wandering around galleries. To Roland, the fitness and art scenes were not worlds apart. Both were the pursuits of the well-off, the lucky ones whose jobs left them enough time to take care of their bodies and to saunter through the arcades of Piccadilly. The lieutenant tried to imagine what John's timetable might have looked like. His job at the agency put him in contact with the idle rich, with whom he might perhaps mingle of an evening at a private view, after stopping off to work on those muscles at the gym. Burny was a hedonist. Roland just had to work out how he satisfied his libido. He had no doubt he went about that artistically too; nothing so conventional as marriage. John had chosen to remain a bachelor. Kate would soon fill him in, Roland hoped. Odds were she had been Burny's mistress herself, at one time or another. Inside the display case, the empty sockets of the skull continued to stare back at Roland. What if John had got involved in trafficking artworks? Perhaps he had tried to double-cross his client? The consequences of that went without saying... Roland picked up his notebook and wrote: Go through victim's bank accounts, trace any transactions to offshore accounts (Isle of Man, Jersey, Barbados). 'Double life of John Burny', the lieutenant added, underlining this part. That was the only possible explanation. The bastard! He was rolling in it. The three thousand pounds cash found in his wallet could only point to a life of crime.

The lieutenant's attention was drawn to the sight of fifty or so people gathered around the entrance to another gallery about a hundred yards further on. The melee was in stark contrast to the reverential hush Roland had experienced in the other art venues. Something must be happening to draw the crowds. Perhaps there was an auction going on? Were they selling off the Crown jewels? Roland wondered, smiling to himself. Buckingham Palace was just down the road. Then it crossed his mind that a crime might have been committed; assuming the worst came with the territory in this job. Yet there were no police officers around. Roland walked over to get a closer look. The people peering towards the entrance hardly seemed afraid. There was a kind of noisy excitement on their faces and in the words streaming out of their mouths. They were anxiously awaiting their turn, guessing how long the wait would be, shouting out, trying to see inside. Roland edged his way round to the back of the queue.

It was an exhibition of contemporary art, or an

installation, to be precise. The building in which the gallery was housed set the tone for what was to come. It was a sort of large windowless cube made of reinforced concrete, slapped in the middle of a Victorian square like a cherry on a cake. It was designed to be unashamedly modern and to look out of place. The queue was moving forward slowly but surely. Five people dove inside the cube whenever five others were let out by another door. By the time he had watched three cohorts make their way in and out, Roland worked out the average visiting time was fifteen minutes. He was nowhere near the front of the queue. The time on his watch read 2 p.m. He had the whole afternoon ahead of him. Rather than get himself lost wandering around town, why not visit this exhibition? It would at least give him something to talk about over dinner with Kate.

The title of the exhibition struck Roland as rather lurid and not especially artistic. A black banner hung across the front of the cube with big red letters screaming 'I love London!' That morning at Victoria, Roland had seen a hawker selling a bundle of T-shirts emblazoned with the same slogan. Perhaps this was what they called street art. One hour on, Roland was beginning to lose patience. Only the sight of the visitors leaving the exhibition kept him from calling it a day. There was an aura of unwholesome pleasure on their faces, like gamblers on slot machines. They came staggering out into the open, gaping-mouthed with a stunned expression in their eyes. They looked absolutely smashed! The visitors came from all walks of life – suits and blue-collar workers, men and women, old and young. Just no kids. Roland turned to look behind him. The queue had doubled. This was the hottest ticket in town.

'I love London!' As he shuffled forward, Roland wondered what exactly the exhibition could be about. Judging by how excited the crowd was, he suspected the worst. Contemporary art often blurred the line with pornography. Embalmed bodies, dismembered naked dolls, photos of horny pubescent teenagers, toothless old women getting their lips round Herculean phalluses, paintings made with shit. There was often not much of a gap between the booming sex trade and the lucrative business of contemporary art, a gap many gallery owners were more than happy to bridge. People came to see 'I love London!' to get an eyeful.

It was finally Roland's turn to go in. A burly-looking bouncer more suited to a nightclub opened and closed the gallery door for the happy few. No sooner had the wide, black-glass door shut behind him than Roland was subjected to an assault of deafening noises, horns blaring, bullets firing and all kinds of explosions (grenades, shells, dynamite). The harsh, blinding light made it impossible to see anything clearly. Above the hullabaloo, a soundtrack was screeching: London is yours.

The lieutenant was bringing up the rear of his group of five. Walking in front of him was an English couple in their forties. They were dressed conservatively, he in a suit and tie, she a straight-fitting skirt cut below the knee. The two men leading the pack were much younger and more interesting to look at. They were the arty sort you would expect to find in a place like this, with ear and nose piercings, tattooed necks, shaved heads, ripped jeans and silk jackets. The exhibition clearly had broad appeal. Yet all responded to it in exactly the same way, covering their ears and widening their eyes to avoid tripping up. The exhibition made an impact right from the start, that was for sure.

Having walked a dozen or so yards to the sound of loudspeakers tirelessly repeating the phrase 'London is yours', the group arrived at a stairwell leading down to an underground level. A glass door stood in their way. After thirty seconds, it magically opened, closing again as soon as the last member of the group had passed through it. As they descended, everything began to change. A low, reddish light illuminated the metal steps and the clang of footsteps echoed off them. The sounds of explosions had ceased, to be replaced by music. Snippets of British pop, from the Beatles to Amy Winehouse by way of the Sex Pistols, alternated with Britten arias in a cacophony mixed by a drunk DJ. The group began to relax, gushing exclamations of delight.

'Amazing! Brilliant! Incredible!' the prim and proper

couple enthused in unison, while the tattooed guys showed their appreciation rather more freely.

'Oh shit! Fucking good!'

Roland was still in shock. '*Merde!*' he thought to himself. 'What the fuck is this place?'

The staircase spiralled down a hundred or so steps before coming to an end at a narrow blue and red glass door which seemed to represent the division between heaven and the underworld. A hidden mechanism operated by an invisible hand unlocked the door to reveal a surprising sight.

A vast space opened up before the visitors in all its glory, and they reacted once again with the same expressions of astonishment. Amazing! Fuck! *Merde!* They didn't know what else to say, overwhelmed at what lay in front of them. The exhibition spanned several different sections of a huge cellar which had been weaved together to form one gothic-style whole. Pillars of black bricks supported three arches cut from obviously fake marble. The place called to mind a torture chamber or catacombs. It was worthy of a Walter Scott novel. Roland was beginning to feel uneasy when his neighbour distracted him by shouting 'Look! The exhibition!'

Five big rectangular tables ran the entire length of the room. A hanging light bulb lit each one, like snooker tables in shady clubs. The installation beneath them was unbelievable. London had been reconstructed area by area with breathtaking precision. Roland immediately recognised St Paul's presiding over the first table, which was dedicated to the City and its surroundings. The second table held Buckingham Palace, bounded by St James's Park to the south and Piccadilly, home to the exhibition, above. Bloomsbury and Trafalgar Square occupied the third table. The chic avenues of Knightsbridge and South Kensington, built in the shadow of Hyde Park, were laid out on the fourth. The fifth followed the curve of the Thames to the white townhouses of Chelsea. Roland looked closely at every table, enthralled. The whole of London seemed to be within his grasp, and the show hadn't even started yet.

A young woman approached the group. Of impressive stature, she was wearing trousers and a black leather jacket zipped down to reveal a glimpse of bare cleavage. She spoke in a theatrical tone, allocating each person to a table. Roland let himself be guided towards table four. Then the woman, who resembled a prison warden more than a museum guide, raised her voice so everyone could hear and shouted: 'Ladies and gentlemen! London is yours!'

The exhibition was in the form of a game. The woman gave a quick summary of the rules. You had to pay to play. Not very much: one pound for one house or block of flats, two pounds for two and so on. With each pound they spent, the player could watch a building be razed to the ground in a puff of white smoke, accompanied by the sound of an explosion. Moments later a brand new structure would emerge from the debris. There were no winners, it was just for fun.

The players got started. The clock was ticking. Several explosions had already rung out by the time Roland got round to putting a coin in the box attached to the underside of the table. The other players hadn't given the money a second thought. Coins rained into the boxes with the clash of metal against steel. To begin with, a few muffled squeals of delight could be heard around the tables. The game had them all hooked. The groans got louder as coins were inserted at a faster and faster rate, building up to a roar of sexual satisfaction when St Paul's collapsed amid a cloud of dust to be replaced a few moments later by a magnificent thirty-storey skyscraper with commanding views over the river and Greater London.

Roland's score remained modest. He didn't know the city. What should he knock down? He wavered for a few moments. A French flag was flying from the facade of a wide building. For one pound sterling he could buy himself the chance to wipe the French embassy off the map. The fear there might be a hidden camera on him dissuaded him from doing it. A little further up, on Kensington Road, a mansion block caught his attention. The old pile seemed to have fallen asleep at the edge of the park. Boom! In a fraction of a second the red bricks had been blasted to pieces and somehow swallowed up by the table in a move Roland was happy to put down to magic. A jaw-dropping luxury residence built of steel, concrete and glass soared up like a Dubai palace, beaming light all around it. High on his success, the lieutenant scrambled to put another coin into the box. Badaboom! Down went the Royal Albert Hall. A fifty-storey tower went up immediately in its place.

Under the vaulted ceiling, the sound of pound coins being frantically thrown at ever greater speed echoed around the room. Each player was rebuilding the city as he or she pleased. 'London is yours', a voice tirelessly whispered. As they pressed the button, they watched open-mouthed with the excitement of wreaking destruction. A good ten minutes had passed since the beginning of the game their hostess had given them fifteen minutes to complete. There was no going over the time limit. Up the stairs and out on the street, others were waiting their turn.

In spite of their thirst for novelty, their desire to see London transformed from top to bottom, the players had barely made a dent in the city's skyline; the vast majority of houses had withstood their voracious appetite for new real estate. Each area still looked much as it had done to start with. White terraced townhouses and red brick mansion blocks continued to leave their mark on the capital. But there was still one last option open to them, which was both costly and radical. For five hundred pounds, you could enjoy the spectacle of total destruction. It was a high price to pay and most players baulked at the idea of taking ten fifties out of their pockets, much as they would have liked to. The game was drawing to an end when the man in the suit and tie called the hostess over by waving his credit card in the air. He wanted total wipeout. Smiling broadly, the young woman came running, clutching the credit card machine. Within seconds his card had been charged. Moments later, he was pressing a red button above which the words 'last game' were written. A deafening roar shook the walls of the room and all eyes were drawn to the table of the champion in a mixture of envy and wonder. He was playing with the City. By a historic irony, the business district sits side by side with the judicial centre of the city. The Law Society is only a few hundred yards away from the Royal Exchange. The law and the markets sum up the spirit of this happy isle. A cloud of smoke rose above a sea of ruins, recalling the Great Fire of 1666. The players were on tenterhooks. What things of wonder would rise from the rubble of the law courts and the stock exchange? What folly? What eccentricity? The smoke gradually cleared to reveal an unexpected sight. Far from the bling of Dubai or the colossal skyscrapers of Shanghai, a bare, sprawling encampment filled the entire space between Tower Bridge and Holborn. Flat-roofed single-storey wooden barracks occupied what was now no more than a vast military zone bordered by the Thames in the south and by high barbed wire-topped fences in the north, east and west. To make it look more realistic, the artist had placed a few tanks here and there, along with little puppets dressed in army fatigues. Just then, a gong rang out to signal the end of the game. The man in the suit undid his tie and unbuttoned his collar. He was white as a sheet. His excitement had abruptly fallen away, like an animal when it has finished mating.

The music had stopped. The woman escorted the players to a lift at the back of the room, hidden behind a heavy curtain. A few moments later they stumbled back out onto the pavement of Piccadilly, wobbly and flushed with pleasure and excitement – all except the businessman, who was still shell-shocked. The crowd waiting outside the entrance had doubled in size, reaching almost riot-like proportions. Tonight the gallery was putting on a night viewing. It would remain open until the early hours of the morning, just like the city's biggest supermarkets, open seven days a week, twenty-four hours a day.

5

It was still two hours before Roland had arranged to meet Kate, and he chose to spend the time in Hyde Park. The warm, flickering autumn light made the Serpentine shimmer with the bronze shades of centuries-old trees. Gazing at the reflections on its surface, Roland recognised his own face smiling ruefully back at him. What momentary madness had brought him to London? Tugged or propelled him there more like. Roland hadn't thought twice about leaving. Staring himself in the face as his reflection became clearer, he was beginning to realise what a mess he had left behind him. He had been so eager to leave, to get the hell out of there, that it was the only thing he had thought about all week; the question of who would win custody of the children hadn't even crossed his mind. That was probably because it had always been obvious to him that Juliette would get to keep them, it occurred to him now. The judge was bound to lay the fault on his side. But wasn't that what he wanted, after all? Sharing the blame meant still sharing something, still being bound to one another, if only by a thread. A gust of cold wind blew over the surface of the water, sweeping aside the autumnal scene and a face stunned at how brutal life could be.

A little way to his left, he was pleased to spot a cafe with tables outside. His throat was dry. A glass of Chablis would go down very nicely. Having queued up at the counter, Roland had to settle for a half-bottle of Argentine Sauvignon. The first glass quenched his thirst, the second made him relax and on the third, he was surprised to find himself thinking about Kate. She turned him on. She was nothing like Juliette. His wife was a woman of principles, ruled by her brain rather than her body. She lacked imagination. Plus she had put weight on, remembered Roland, forgetting that the same was true of him. Kate was a little younger than Juliette, or at least he thought she probably was. She looked somewhere between thirty and thirty-five. In any case, she seemed determined never to look her age. There was something overtly sexual about her that made her instantly desirable. And didn't she know it. She would still be giving men hard-ons at the age of fifty, Roland had no doubt about that. He ran his hand over the top of his trousers. His dick was hard. 'What the fuck am I doing here?' he asked himself again, but this time the answer was clear to see.

Roland looked at his watch. It would soon be time to get back to his hotel if he wanted to have a shower before going to meet Kate. Then he checked his mobile phone. Samy had left him a voicemail. He was asking for an update. London, the hotel, the estate agency Roland had told him about before leaving Paris. How was it all going? He ended the message by asking Roland to call Juliette, with whom he had spoken on the phone. He didn't elaborate. Call her. It's the right thing to do. Surprised to hear his wife had been in touch with his deputy, Roland dialled Juliette's number only to hang up again almost immediately.

Roland found Kate glued to her computer screen when he entered her office.

'I'll be two minutes,' she shouted without looking up.

She was waiting for him to arrive, the lieutenant told himself. He walked towards her desk, trying to behave appropriately for the circumstances, though what exactly those circumstances were wasn't quite clear. Officially he was here to talk about John. The context of his visit was the murder inquiry. Roland cast a cursory glance at the wall-mounted screens on which pictures of various properties had been displayed that morning. They were all turned off now. The agency had been closed for an hour.

'Are you searching the office for clues?'

The note of irony in the question caught Roland off guard. Before he had time to think of a comeback, Kate was standing in front of him.

'Ready!'

She was smiling. Her freshly made-up lips wore a smile that was just so: casual and polite, seductive and reserved. She knew what she was doing. Roland couldn't help but smile back, spellbound. Mission accomplished. Her gaze followed that of the lieutenant as he undressed her with his eyes. She had got changed, discarding her jeans in favour of a black mini skirt which showed off the curve of her thighs. On her feet she wore a pair of white leather stilettos, which she walked in as easily and naturally as if they were merely an extension of her legs. There was more to admire, but Roland thought it best to stop looking for fear of coming across as too keen, or ridiculous, in other words. Just a quick appreciative glance, as if to say, 'I know what you're doing and I like it.' Kate's greatest charm was the way she invited you in on her trick the moment you found her out. Looking at her meant playing along with her. The only alternative was to avert your eyes and keep walking like a puritan.

'So how's your investigation going?' asked Kate after the waitress at the restaurant, a Thai place just down the road from the office, had set down their bottle of red Sancerre. It was only just getting started, the lieutenant explained, but he couldn't go into too much detail about what he was doing in London. Kate understood, of course. Then she began grilling him on the circumstances of the tragedy, making him run through the events of the night for the hundredth time. Kate had seen the stories in the papers about the English couple's mistreatment at the hands of the French police; their picture was splashed across all the front pages. It was an absolute disgrace, in her opinion. But the violence of the French police – and of the French full stop, she added emphatically – was well known. Kate judged the French to be a rather boorish breed. Of course they were the experts when it came to wine and fine food, but they had a lot to learn about good manners. Gradually the conversation turned to the relative merits of both countries. Clichés were bandied around left right and centre. The famous British courtesy was just for show, in Roland's view. An iron fist inside a velvet glove. As far as Kate was concerned, the French obsession with taking to the streets at the slightest grievance summed up what a nation of complainers they were. Both of them took equal pleasure in reeling off the most well-worn commonplaces. They kept the conversation going, because talking brought them closer to one another. On two occasions Roland felt Kate's leg brushing against his trousers. They went on and on talking, almost without paying attention to what they were saying. The only subject they were careful to avoid, by tacit agreement, was John Burny. Death was not a suitable topic for the dinner table. Besides, the agreeable ambiance of the restaurant, with its soft lighting and colonial-style decor, was more conducive to relaxation than conducting a criminal inquiry. Ultimately Roland was able to convince himself that by getting closer to Kate, he was getting closer to John. The bill had just arrived.

'Voilà, this is me!' she said a little later, pushing open the front door of the Victorian building in which she lived.

Like John, Kate lived just around the corner from the agency. But the similarity ended there. Burny owned a ground floor flat. As for Kate: 'We own the house,' she said, turning on the light in the entrance hall. It was the first time over the course of the evening she had mentioned this 'we', which she employed like a defensive weapon. 'We bought it almost ten years ago, before prices went through the roof.'

Still, the not-so-humble three-storey abode must have cost a pretty penny even then, thought Roland, gazing around the living room Kate had just led him into. Having dropped the husband into the conversation without further explanation, Kate was now flaunting her wealth, which Roland thought best to pass over without comment. She was putting him in his place. He would soon find out what place that was. She disappeared for a moment before strutting back in holding a drink in each hand. They made a toast to the *entente cordiale* and both took a large swig of gin and tonic. Without pausing for breath, Kate planted a kiss on the lieutenant's alcohol-warmed lips.

'Feeling horny?' she asked him.

*

There's a lot to be said for mathematics. It never gets it wrong. Lying on the bed in the guest room, Kate was flexing her wrists, relieved. She had just finished demonstrating her proof and it had all added up nicely.

'Does it hurt?' Roland asked after setting her free.

'No. Not really. It just pinches a bit,' Kate replied, turning to look at the lieutenant, her pupils dilated with satisfaction.

The pleasure Roland had felt rising up at the dinner table, only to be knocked back with that word 'we' and all that ostentatious wealth, the pleasure that had suddenly returned on contact with Kate's lips, that he had been anticipating all evening and all day, ever since leaving the estate agency, the pleasure he had been yearning for had been fulfilled to him with an arithmetic accuracy that blew his mind, even if it had arrived in a shape he had not seen coming.

Kate had not needed to spell it out for him. She had simply wiggled a pair of handcuffs before the lieutenant's hungry eyes and added, 'Let's play.'

The script had been written and everyone knew their lines. Roland surprised himself with his aptitude for the role. He began by shoving Kate backwards onto the bed before handcuffing her to the frame. She put up a fight, thrashing with all her might to throw off the advances of the shady cop character, thereby heightening her own enjoyment as well as that of her partner in crime. 'Bad lieutenant,' she said over and again between groans of pleasure. They came together.

'Where exactly?' he asked.

Kate took hold of Roland's hand and placed it against the underside of her wrist.

'Here. Right there.'

He began gently massaging the spot where the metal cuffs had left a faint red mark on the tanning-booth bronzed skin. Kate half-closed her eyes and gave in to the sensation. She looked even sexier like this than she had while tied up. Was this intentional? Was she playing a new game? Roland kept rubbing, moving on to the other wrist and stroking his hand up and down the firm, silky-smooth skin of her arms. Kate was naked. She had now taken off the black skirt, which she had kept on during sex. She turned Roland on without even trying, and he found himself wanting to chain her up again but for real this time, to get her to repeat the experience she seemed to have lost interest in carrying on. Lo and behold, as he went to move her hand back in the direction of the bed frame, Kate squirmed away from him and jumped out of bed like a cat. He was offered one last drink out of politeness, which he consumed joylessly before leaving. It was like Kate said at dinner. Politeness is the virtue of the English.

Back at his hotel, Roland didn't go to sleep until well into the night, having stayed up watching a Ken Loach film called *It's a Free World* on pay TV.

*

Juliette Desfeuillères had kissed the children goodbye and repeated her instructions to the new babysitter. She was going out for the night. She had decided to change her childcare arrangements in order to avoid the questions the regular babysitter would inevitably have asked about Roland. And how's Monsieur Desfeuillères? On duty tonight then, is he? Juliette couldn't have faced it. For the last ten days or so she had been struggling to get by living in some kind of bad dream that made absolutely no sense to her. Roland's departure fell into the realm of the absurd. The request for a divorce received the previous day had sent her reeling. That night at the dinner table fielding Ludivine and Corentin's barrage of questions, she tried in vain to think of a reason for this crazy situation. Another woman? She would have known about it. An age thing? That might be part of it, but she would expect him to have ummed and ahhed about it first. Men dither in such situations, pick fights and then back out of them. She and he had almost never fought but for the odd little disagreement, as she saw them. No arguments until the bizarre scene that Friday which had ended with Roland walking out in the middle of the night – like a dog, she said to herself, enraged at her inability to stop him, wondering how she could have been stupid enough not to see it coming.

'Maman! When's papa coming home?' Ludivine kept asking.

'Maman! Where's papa gone?' Corentin would chime in.

In the space of ten days, from the moment she had woken up on the Saturday morning and searched high and low for her husband, as though he might be hiding under a table or in a cupboard, until the Monday morning of the following week when she got the phone call from the lawyer informing her of her husband's decision, as if he were incapable of letting her know himself, face to face, in a cafe or restaurant or something, I don't know, we could have talked it over, maybe I could have made some sense of it, said something back to him, made him see reason, instead of hanging on the end of the line like a fucking idiot while Maître Vlaminck stuffed his cold words and talk of proceedings down my throat, insisting on saying 'my client' and not Roland or your husband, in barely ten days Juliette had watched her life descend into a nightmare. And the fact she kept using the word 'nightmare' meant she still held out some hope of escaping from it. It couldn't be true. Sooner or later she would wake up.

This evening she was taking the first steps towards enlightenment. Juliette could not accept her husband's decision without understanding it. The idea that there might be nothing to understand was unfathomable. She had to find someone with a manual to explain how this new bloke worked, this person hiding behind her husband's familiar face. She hadn't had to spend long looking. Roland had often mentioned his new deputy, who was still young and had just pitched up from Marseilles. Tonight she was on her way to meet him.

There wasn't much traffic on Rue des Pyrénées and the taxi dropped her slightly early outside the bistro on Rue Lafayette where Samy Bouallem had suggested they meet at eight thirty. It was only just twenty past. What should she do? Juliette was annoyed at being the first to arrive. She wished she hadn't rushed to be ready on time; in the past she had always managed to be five or eight minutes late. Standing outside the restaurant, she was forced to admit that she was out of the habit of going out during the week. She had become set in her ways. She wondered then if that wasn't what Roland had been running away from: a life of predictability. It wasn't her he was rejecting but the lifestyle they had fallen into. Perhaps all was not lost after all.

Reassured by this thought, she pushed open the door to the restaurant. Most of the tables were free. She asked the waiter for a table for two. One by the window.

'A kir, please.'

Right then. Here she was. She sat waiting. What would she call the sub-lieutenant? Samy? She had never met him before. Monsieur Bouallem? That was a bit formal. Lieutenant? No way. 'I'll know what to say when the time comes.' She smiled at her own uncertainty and took a gulp of her aperitif. At this time on a weeknight, there weren't many people around on Rue Lafayette.

Juliette tried in vain to find something interesting to look at. The road seemed desperately empty, like a reflection of her own existence. 'What the hell am I doing here?' she suddenly asked herself. She found the answer in her memory. Or rather, she didn't have to find it. It had simply come to her while she continued to stare into space. It was already more than a fortnight ago. It seemed like an eternity. Her life with Roland was spinning away from her at uncontrollable speed. In fact, it was exactly a week before he walked out. Roland had come home late that night. She had just put the kids to bed. He had grabbed hold of her in the corridor as she was trying to reach the living room, feeling tired and fed up at having to wait around for her husband on an almost daily basis. His grip was tight, and it seemed as though he meant to hurt her. She dropped the book she had been holding, suddenly afraid, no longer recognising the man she loved in the person who stood before her. 'I don't understand him anymore.'

'Madame Desfeuillères?'

Juliette lifted her head, taken aback, anxious that her thoughts might somehow be written on her face.

'Samy Bouallem.'

'Pleased to meet you,' she replied, collecting herself.

As he took off his jacket and hung it off the back of the chair, she watched him out of the corner of her eye. He moved naturally and exuded an aura of warmth. She immediately felt at ease.

The dinner – a light, simple affair – was drawing to a close, and they had barely touched on Roland. The sub-lieutenant didn't know his superior very well. His boss didn't open up very often, even though the two of them had had lunch together many times. Desfeuillères sometimes referred to his happy home life in broad terms: two fantastic children, a wonderful wife. Bouallem knew nothing about their quarrel.

'It's more than a quarrel,' Juliette corrected him. 'He's asking for a divorce.'

Samy was gobsmacked – as was Juliette, for that matter. They were joined by their shared inability to understand what had happened. Desfeuillères had betrayed their trust.

'He could have told me before he buggered off to London,' cried Samy.

That was it, in terms of talk about the lieutenant. They had, however, spoken a great deal about themselves, their youth and the paths they had taken. They were the same age, give or take a few months.

In the taxi taking her back home, Juliette felt herself relaxing for the first time in ten days. She began to breathe more easily. She felt a little less alone in the face of her problems. Samy – as she had happily called him throughout the meal – seemed like a nice guy. She had perhaps said too much: that was her one regret about the evening. But she had felt such a need to talk about it all. She hadn't yet told any of her friends what had happened, hoping and praying that everything would return to normal before they knew anything was wrong. Roland was bound to come back. When he had told her on Saturday that he would be spending the night in a hotel, she had assumed it would be a one-off. There was no doubt in her mind he would be back first thing the next day. When Sunday passed without a phone call, she realised it was more serious than she'd thought. On Monday, she left a message on his mobile. 'We need to talk.' She awoke on Tuesday morning to find a message Roland must have left during the night. The same thing happened several times over the next few days. She could never get hold of him, and he would call her back when she was asleep. The call from the lawyer yesterday had knocked her sideways. In less than ten days, Juliette had gone through a thousand subtly different emotions, from the mildest to the most extreme, but had told no one about any of it for fear of being unduly influenced or poorly advised, and, superstitious in spite of herself, afraid of tempting fate. As the taxi headed back up Rue des Pyrénées, the thought of the past few painful days gradually gave way to the memory of the evening she had just had. Juliette was pleased to have taken the bull by the horns. She and Samy had agreed to meet again in a few days if Roland still wasn't back, to assess the situation. Samy seemed as concerned as she was.

Nothing of John Burny's was missing, or almost

nothing. The day after the murder, having made numerous fruitless attempts to reach Interpol, Lieutenant Desfeuillères had meticulously sorted through the victim's personal effects: small leather travel bag, designer clothes, travel documents. The whole lot had been thrown carelessly into a standard bin bag. The wallet seemed to be intact: bank cards (Burny had two, a debit card and credit card), various loyalty cards, business cards, passport and finally cash. Roland's inspection of the clothes and luggage hadn't thrown much up either. Burny could have been any other traveller coming to live it up in Paris. The presence of a box of condoms seemed to confirm the theory that he was out for a good time. There was, however, one key object missing, or at least one that most people now considered an essential. Burny didn't have a phone on him. Had he left it behind in London? Had it been stolen? In that case, why wouldn't the thief have taken the wad of cash bulging out of the wallet too? Might he have been disturbed? Unlikely. In a hurry? He had to remember this was not a simple case of theft, but a murder. Perhaps the victim's phone held sensitive information.

This telephone, if indeed there was one, must also contain a list of contacts and probably a large number of messages. Who had been waiting for Burny in Paris? Had they tried to call him when there had been no sign of him at the station? But perhaps there was no one expecting him after all? The lack of mobile phone added to the impression of Burny as an isolated character. A friendless, aimless loner, who had got on a train one day and never got off again.

Still half asleep, Desfeuillères stood waiting in the reception area of a makeshift police station situated on the fourth floor of a concrete building. There was nothing smart about the place. Lawyers, insurance brokers, various haulage companies and other businessmen rubbed shoulders over six floors of nondescript building in a nondescript part of south London, somewhere around Lewisham. The lieutenant had been anticipating an altogether different kind of welcome. To him, the word 'Interpol' conjured up an image of British greatness which he associated with the name of Sherlock Holmes. But he had to face facts. He was trapped in a shabby fourth floor waiting area, surrounded by dirty grey walls. He had a sneaking suspicion he was being led up the garden path.

And his British colleague was late, to boot. The surly girl at the front desk, old before her time, had curtly informed him of this on his arrival. Sir Ranesh Ashaniravaya was stuck in traffic. He would be there in fifteen or twenty minutes. Then she had politely invited Roland to sit in one of the three metal chairs that furnished the room. The receptionist's tone, the tatty appearance of the place and the tardiness of the man he had arranged to meet all served to back up his first impression. He was not being taken seriously.

The miserable weather wasn't exactly helping matters. It had been drizzling all day, casting an air of gloom over the city. Looking out of the window, Roland could see dozens of umbrellas fighting for space on the pavement below. They formed a dull, dark stain on the rain-soaked roadway. The bright red double-deckers stopping to pick up the swarms of umbrella-holders were the only splashes of colour livening up the scene. Dull, low red-brick buildings housed cheap corner shops whose shelves were lined with pre-packaged sandwiches and cleaning products. Roland suddenly missed Paris, its Haussmann-era architecture, delicatessens, brasseries, and not forgetting Juliette, of course. 'What the hell am I doing here?' he asked himself, frustrated. He turned his back on the road, the greyness of which was getting him down. He now faced the girl at the reception desk, who was filing her nails in an open display of boredom. Confusingly, since Roland had witnessed no one coming or going, she then made a feeble announcement to the effect that Sir Ranesh Ashaniravaya had entered the building:

'He's waiting for you in his office.'

'Which door is it?' asked Roland.

'End of the corridor, fourth on the left.'

As it turned out, the name Roland feared he would not be able to pronounce was written in italics on the door at the end of the corridor, underneath the words 'CRIMINAL INVESTIGATION DEPARTMENT' etched into the glass in big capital letters. Underneath, very small, you could just make out the word 'Detective'.

'Ranesh. Call me Ranesh,' the young man said as Roland pushed open the door of his office. He was of Indian descent, with remarkably matte skin and smart civilian clothing. His smile looked put-on and his tone was excessively friendly. Without ado, he began to question the French lieutenant on the way in which he was conducting his inquiry.

'May I ask what it is you've come to London to find out?'

Though it had been put perfectly politely, the question was rather abrupt and caught Roland off guard. He had been expecting some preliminary chat about France or Paris, how his journey had gone, what he thought of London. He had prepared a few words of small talk to get the conversation flowing. But Ranesh was making him get straight to the point.

'Would you allow me to ask if you are following any particular lead?'

Having met with an uncomfortable silence, Ranesh refocused his questions on the circumstances of the crime, forcing Roland to tell the same story he had recounted so many times before. The tables were being turned. Roland had come here to get information from a colleague and now it was him being put in the hot seat and treated like an amateur. The British man was taking him for a fool. Roland was struggling to contain his annoyance, which was heightened further when Ranesh placed a document in front of him stating that the crime had been committed on French soil, and asked him to sign it. The rest appeared to be a matter of no importance. And the rest concerned John Burny.

'Who was he?' Roland finally got the chance to ask.

'If I may speak frankly, John Burny seems to have been an entirely unblemished character,' said Ranesh breezily.

'A charming man, then, you'd say?' pressed the lieutenant, whose exasperation was written on his face.

'Yes. That's exactly it. A charming man. You guessed it,' replied Ranesh, a smile playing on his lips.

'So what could anyone have possibly held against him, to the point of murdering him?' Roland continued. 'Because this is a murder we're talking about. That's the problem we have here.'

'I'm going to smack him in the face if he carries on treating me like a fucking idiot,' he was thinking.

'You're quite right. Without wishing to force your hand, it seems to me you've come to London to shed light on this crime, if I'm not overstepping the mark. We're counting on you.'

The young man was standing a fair distance across the room. He had not changed his position since Roland walked in and found him there. Expressing no trace of emotion, he looked like a robot specially made for the occasion. He appeared to be incapable of deviating even slightly from his ready-prepared script. He was driving the lieutenant up the wall. 'I'll get him to talk,' he told himself. Burny must have been a person of some importance to be receiving this level of protection. Roland was becoming sure of it. There was an affair of State behind all this.

'Might you by any chance,' asked Roland, adopting Ranesh's tone and manners, 'have something, some clue that might point my inquiry in one direction more than another?'

'Yes,' replied Ranesh with a Buddha-like grin, 'there may well be something worth dwelling on. But I couldn't say for certain. I was in two minds whether to bring it up, it seemed so insignificant.'

'Please, go ahead.'

'If you insist. I was unaware of this myself until yesterday. The file didn't land on my desk until late in the evening. Our intelligence services have been working flat-out. You're aware of our reputation, I'm sure.'

He was striding up and down the room. Though he kept looking at Roland, his eyes were vacant. Their gaze seemed to pass straight through the lieutenant to stare at some imaginary object, which could just as easily be Her Majesty the Queen as the dish he was dreaming of having for lunch.

'Here it is,' he continued after pausing for a few

moments, as if reluctant to say the words. 'Here's what the file told me. John Burny was very often to be found at Soho's gay clubs.'

'You're telling me now that John Burny was homosexual!' cried the lieutenant, gobsmacked.

'I haven't said or implied anything of the sort,' said Ranesh by way of response, his smile now having morphed into an expression of distaste. 'I'm simply giving you the facts as they stand. It's not for me to pass comment. And since your curiosity seems not to have been satisfied, let me add that the file also said that the victim had regularly been seen in the company of young people. Very young people, in fact.'

'He was a paedophile?' the lieutenant exclaimed even more incredulously, now mirroring the look of disgust on the face of the man he was speaking to. The two men finally appeared to be in tune with one another.

But what about Kate? wondered Roland. How could she have been Burny's mistress if he was gay? He suddenly realised Kate had never told him any such thing. In fact she had never told him anything at all about John, other than that he was a charming man. Yeah, right, what a charmer. Now it turned out he was a paedophile. Unless this guy was having him on.

'Certainly not!' Ranesh replied indignantly. 'According to my file, Burny was careful to abide by the age of consent. There's no suggestion he ever broke the law.'

'Still, the guy doesn't sound as charming as all that, if I follow your meaning!' pointed out the lieutenant, taken aback at his colleague's comments.

'His behaviour was perfectly legal,' replied Ranesh simply. 'What else can I say? We have no business rebuking a citizen for what he chooses to do within the confines of the law.'

'Do you think we might have a lead with this?'

Roland's use of the word 'we' shocked the Englishman more than the question itself.

'There's nothing stopping you following it up,' he replied, putting the emphasis on the word 'you'.

'Another comment like that and I'll send him flying at the wall,' the lieutenant told himself, approaching boiling point. 'My God I'd like to thump him.' Yet he managed to calm himself down, aware that such an act would fall 'outside the confines of the law' of this country where rules were followed to the letter. As for the rest of it, as Ranesh had pointed out, everyone was free to do as they chose.

'Can you point me in the direction of any of these places, so I can start looking into them?' asked the lieutenant. Receiving no response, he was forced to make himself clearer. 'I expect you know the names of one or two of the gay bars Burny used to frequent.'

'Of course not!' It was the Englishman's turn to express irritation at the pointed use of the word 'you'.

As he prepared to ask another question, Ranesh cut

him off and began leading him towards the door.

'I'll leave you to get on with your work,' he said by way of farewell. 'If I can be of any assistance at all, please don't hesitate to give me a call. You have my number.'

There had been a change in the weather. When, a few moments later, Roland stepped out into the square in front of the building, the road was bathed in bright sunshine.

The next day, Desfeuillères got down to business. The previous evening, after swinging by the gym, he had spent an hour or so laying out his plan of action, which revolved around five key points: 1) go through Burny's Barclays accounts with a fine-tooth comb; 2) search the victim's flat; 3) get hold of the list of passengers who were on board the ill-fated train ('big job' he underlined in the margin of his notebook); 4) investigate real estate transactions: Burny might have been caught up in one or more fraudulent operations involving backhanders or dirty money; 5) check out the information Ranesh had given him about John's sexual orientation and, if need be, take the investigation to Soho ('be discreet' he underlined twice in the margin).

The to-do list was by no means exhaustive. New information could crop up which could lead the inquiry off in any number of directions. Nevertheless, the list gave Roland something to work with, and in that sense it was proving useful. It gave him a framework to build his days around, up until the following Tuesday. He had given himself a week to gain some insight into the case. The order in which the tasks were to be completed was not set in stone. In fact it was bound to change, depending on how well he got on with each task, and how long each of them took. His ability to tick them off would depend in large part upon other people's willingness to help. He would no doubt have a hard time getting anything out of the train company, for example. Aviation companies, train companies, shippers, insurers, in fact companies of all kinds are always reluctant to reveal the identities of their members, partners or passengers. The business world has kept a taste for secrets, in spite of society's greater openness: a kind of monarchic throwback in an age of enlightenment. Roland also expected to meet with resistance from estate agents, but thankfully he had Kate on side. He picked up his pencil and added to the list: 6) contact Kate ('quickly' underlined three times).

John Burny banked at a small local branch in the shadow of Victoria station, on the corner of a narrow road that was difficult to find. Burny could drop in on his way to work or even between viewings, it occurred to the lieutenant as he pushed open the door and stepped inside the bank, which was empty at this time of the morning. He walked straight up to the only counter that was open, without bothering to wait behind the blue line marked on the floor. The cashier, a young woman in a black headscarf, immediately gestured to him to step back, before pointing discreetly at the sign near the entrance which read 'Please wait to be served'. Five minutes later, a pre-recorded voice informed Roland he could go to cashier number three. The girl, suddenly smiling, bright and professional, asked how she could help him.

In a matching tone of voice, but with a forced smile that didn't escape the girl's notice, Roland told her he wanted to speak to the manager. Her smile dropped. The manager didn't talk to customers willy-nilly. Roland kept trying. He was happy to make an appointment and come back later. The girl stood firm. Did Monsieur Desfeuillères have a Barclays account? Or would he like to open one today? She would be more than happy to help. The lieutenant raised his voice. He *absolutely must* see the manager.

'Thank you, sir,' was the response.

The girl simultaneously pressed a button to play the automated message. The next customer could go to cashier number three. Roland turned round. There was no one behind him. At that point, he took out his French police ID and waved it in front of the anxious-looking cashier. No, of course he didn't have an account at Barclays but John Burny had and he had been murdered. Despite the fact she was protected behind a thick sheet of bulletproof glass, the girl shrank back in her chair as if she was being threatened. She looked stunned. Once again she played the automated announcement before pressing another button. Seconds later a burly security guard came rushing out, grabbed the lieutenant by the arm and bundled him towards the exit. Just before he was pushed out the door, Roland heard the automatic voice repeat its refrain one more time.

Once he had brushed himself off, Roland decided to call Ranesh. He was the only one who could help him. An artificial voice answered, inviting him to leave a message. Roland hung up, furious. It was 9.30 a.m. He had been thrown out of Barclays and Ranesh was nowhere to be found. The day had not exactly started well, and it was shaping up to be long and fruitless. The timetable he had carefully drawn up in his hotel room the night before was going up in smoke. Should he call Kate? Now was not the time. Head up to St Pancras to see the train company? 'They'll tell me where to stick it just as politely as the rest of them,' the lieutenant fumed, feeling angry with himself. He was going about this like a rookie. Not that there was much he could do about it. He called Ranesh again but this time left a message in which he did his utmost to sound polite and friendly. Roland was beginning to bend to the customs of the kingdom.

Now what? he wondered. The air was cool but dry. A timid sun – a 'polite' sun, one might say – was shining sweetly on Terminus Place at the front of Victoria station. With his head in the sky, Roland didn't notice the passer-by who accidentally bumped into him and immediately apologised, wearing a look of genuine regret: 'I'm so sorry.' It was now 9.40 a.m. He had to bounce back, and fast. As he saw it, he had two options: 1) Look around London. North, south, east or west: he only had to choose, since he had still done almost no sightseeing. But it wasn't the time for that. He wasn't here as a tourist. In any case he couldn't really be bothered. 2) Go to the gym. He had already dropped in the day before. He had hung around the changing rooms for a while, sniffing about, keeping an eye, trying to strike up a conversation before eventually chickening out; he wasn't very familiar with these sorts of places, nor with the types of people who spent time there. He finished his tour in the weights room. There was no avoiding doing some exercise in here, 1, 2, 1, 2, for half an hour or so, long enough to make it look like he was really doing a work-out, as he kept telling himself with each lift of the dumbbell. Yes, that was it: he needed to go back to the gym. There was really no substitute for investigating on the ground. Things were looking up. He just had to swing by the hotel to pick up the sports kit he had bought the day before in a shop on Piccadilly.

The lieutenant was warming up on the running machine. He had been at it for a quarter of an hour, running with short, regular strides, remembering to breathe in and out, but already struggling. His calves and thighs were showing signs of fatigue. Sweat was collecting under his armpits, forming unpleasant patches on the sleeves of his T-shirt. 'Don't stop,' he kept telling himself, 'Don't give up too soon.' 'One more,' he said to himself each time he completed a lap, 'Just one more.' The physical exertion had gradually developed into physical pain. He hurt all over. His heart was beating too fast. One last lap. It was so good to feel his body hold up under the pain. 'There. Almost there. I'll slow it down, ease off towards the end.'

The sports gear he was wearing was already soaked through. The previous day he had spent a long time deciding whether or not to buy a new kit and then debating which style to go for. But firstly, as he reminded himself firmly in order to force himself into one of those sports shops whose customers are almost exclusively under the age of twenty, he didn't really have a choice. And secondly, there was no point scrimping on it if he wanted to fit in with the members, who after all lived in one of London's most exclusive postcodes. He further deliberated over the choice of colour before opting for a pair of white shorts with two fluorescent green stripes, teamed with a vest in a shade of green which seemed to him subtle and understated compared with the ones in crazy colours (orange and yellow, red with gold stripes, black and bright yellow) which made you look like a road sign. A pair of trainers suitable for weight training and strongly recommended by the shop assistant put the finishing touch to the outfit.

Roland was finding it difficult to recover from his exertion. He leant against the wall and stretched the muscles in his legs. His tendons were burning. On his right was a huge mirror, which made the room look bigger at the same time as flattering the gym bunnies. You could admire yourself as you exercised. It was a competition to see who was the most attractive. Roland couldn't help but examine his reflection. His face was red and puffed out. The image before him was of a man who was worn out. He looked five years older than his age. The mirror never lied. He had his work cut out if he was ever going to get a toned body to rival John Burny's. The bastard! Roland tried to calculate how many work-outs it would take to get back in shape. If he went to the gym three times a week and did a range of different exercises, he might get himself back to the appropriate weight for his height within about four weeks. The bulging biceps and six-pack might have to wait until the New Year, say, or the fourth of never. 'I'm losing it,' he said to himself. Roland was only in London for the week. If he really pushed it, he might convince the prosecutor to allow him another week. Three would be ideal, but for that he would need a compelling line of inquiry. In any case, Roland had no desire to return to Paris that Sunday. He looked at himself in the mirror again. The belly was the issue. Three weeks, not a day less.

'You shouldn't be wearing those shoes for running. They'll knacker your legs.'

Roland jumped, as if caught naked. Standing in front of him was a tall young man who carried on talking without waiting for a response:

'You see,' he said, pointing to Roland's calves. 'They're all swollen.'

Roland had indeed been experiencing a dull ache which had begun in the Achilles tendon and was spreading up his leg. The initial buzz of feeling his body push itself was now switching to a sense of unease.

'You were close to breaking point there.'

Breaking point? Roland automatically placed his hand against his heart. It was beating very quickly, too quickly perhaps. His temples also seemed to be throbbing. Before he had time to react, the young man knelt down beside him and placed a hand on his calf.

'There. The muscle was close to snapping.'

Roland let himself breathe again. How stupid he had been! Drop dead here? He felt like laughing. But he jumped a second time when the guy started massaging his leg with firm yet gentle strokes of the hand. Roland hadn't yet said a word to him, not even a hello. He had been struck dumb the moment the man first spoke to him. The situation was getting out of hand. The guy must be at least six foot three. He was half a head taller than Roland, or so it seemed for the short time he had stood level with him, for now that the man was absorbed in his task, his two hands squeezing Roland's calves, stroking the backs of his knees and slowly easing up his thighs; now that he was kneeling at Roland's feet with his head bowed, it was hard to say exactly how much taller he was than him.

'How's that, better? I'm David.'

'Roland. Yes. That helps.'

'Pleased to meet you, Roland. I really thought you might pass out there. Take it easy next time.'

The whole time he was talking, David carried on massaging the lieutenant's legs. The latter found himself enjoying it; the former too, for that matter. But Roland, who had initially found the sense of release brought on by David's expert touch perfectly natural, was beginning to feel uncomfortable as the simple physical relief morphed into a more muddled cloud of emotions. He thought it best to put an end to the impromptu massage session and pointedly looked down at his watch.

'Oh, it's twelve thirty. Must dash.'

David let his hands fall to his sides, making no attempt to mask his disappointment. He gazed up questioningly at Roland.

'New to the gym?'

'Yes. A friend recommended I try it,' replied Desfeuillères, who had just remembered what it was he was supposed to be doing here.

'I probably know him. I know pretty much everyone

here. I'm the masseur. David McLoggin.'

He searched the back pocket of his shorts and handed Roland a crumpled business card.

'Does the name John Burny mean anything to you?'

Despite his best efforts, Roland had reverted to an interrogatory tone. He feared he might already have raised David's suspicions. But David had got to his feet at the mere mention of John Burny's name, paying no attention to the way the question had been phrased. He pinned his deep blue eyes on Roland with an expression of disbelief. He towered a good head above him.

'You knew John?' he asked, his voice wavering.

'We used to meet up sometimes when he came to Paris,' said Roland, having decided to fabricate a story.

'Do you know what happened to him?'

'Yes, I'm afraid I do!' cried the lieutenant, trying to sound suitably devastated. 'It's so awful. I still can't believe it.'

David had reacted very strongly to the mention of John's name. Perhaps Roland was on to something here. Now it was his turn to look David straight in the eyes. The masseur was still staring at him, but his expression was less candid. He appeared less sure of himself, and a thin veil of sadness fell over his gaze like a cloud drifting across a blue sky. Then he pulled himself together. He had things to be getting on with too, he said. Now Roland was regretting having jumped the gun. His first real lead was slipping through his fingers. David was already walking away. Roland was going to call after him to suggest going for a drink, when David turned back.

'Call me whenever you like. My number's on my card.'

'Tomorrow?' Roland shot back.

'Why not tonight? Give me a ring after eight o'clock.'

After showering and getting changed, the lieutenant checked his mobile phone. There was a message from Ranesh. 'Call me back,' it was now his turn to ask. Roland dialled his number immediately, only to reach his answer phone once again. Was Ranesh playing games with him? This time Roland left a long and detailed message. It was not until the end of the afternoon that Ranesh called back. He had made the necessary call to Barclays. Roland could return to the branch tomorrow and would be given access to John Burny's accounts. Ranesh had not managed to get hold of the boss of the train company, however; he was a busy man, he pointed out to justify his failure. Roland wouldn't give up that easily. That list was a crucial element of the inquiry.

'I'm aware of that,' Ranesh admitted, before backpedalling. The lieutenant wouldn't get anywhere without permission from the MD, Sir Alvaro Barbossa. Unfortunately he was out of the country at the moment.

'Of course,' he added, 'Someone who runs a train company would travel a lot.'

At the other end of the line, Roland was beginning to fume. Ranesh seemed to have a knack for winding him up. When would the MD be back? Ranesh had no idea. Sir Alvaro Barbossa was in Shanghai. An important deal.

'Breaking China is big business, as I'm sure you can imagine.'

'Well maybe his deputy could help me out,' pressed Roland.

At that point Ranesh lost his temper. He couldn't understand why his colleague was so set on this idea.

'You do realise,' he said, 'how unlikely it is that the murderer travelled under his own name. You'll get nothing out of checking up on everyone on the passenger list. You'll be wasting precious time.'

Roland gradually came to the conclusion he was being told to pack it in, as Ranesh went into great detail about all the obstacles standing in the way of the endeavour, and all the reasons why it would never work. Ranesh seemed in a hurry to hang up. But Roland still had one last request to make. He wanted to carry out a search of John's flat.

'Oh! No problem!' cried the British detective, whose tone had suddenly softened. 'I'll have the keys dropped off at your hotel tomorrow morning, OK?'

'Perfect!'

But Ranesh had already hung up. Right, thought Roland, placing a calming hand against his brow. 1) Barclays, 2) John's flat. But before either of those things, he must call David.

6

Juliette was waiting for the metro at Gambetta station. It was early on a Saturday evening and the platform was packed. It had been a nice afternoon. Considering it was now the first of October, the autumn had been mild so far. The warm light made you forget that the Earth turns in only one direction. The train was running late. Juliette glanced at her watch. Nothing to worry about. Still, she felt ever so slightly anxious, but dismissed this with the voice of a woman well used to examining the pleats and folds of her own conscience. She had got dressed up for this evening. She was wearing a summer dress she had dug out from the back of the wardrobe. She thought it suited the occasion; it was sexy, and it still fitted. She smiled at her own vanity; it was girlish of her to care so much.

Her mind was buzzing. 'To think that a week ago I was hoping everything would go back to the way it was. Heroine of a romantic novel.' To get from Gambetta to Montparnasse, where Juliette was heading, you had to allow between thirty and forty minutes. Changing at Réaumur, it might be more like forty-five. 'I'm going to be late. Ten minutes or so, not much more. He'll wait for me this time.' The train had just arrived. It was empty. Seconds later the carriages were filling up with a good-natured crowd of evening revellers. Juliette slid between two groups of teenagers to get to a seat. 'I was hoping for a happy ending. That's how I pictured it. A happy ending. Always had my head in the clouds, read too many books. What's the word I'm looking for? Roland. Keep telling myself it can't be any other way. One phone call in two weeks. First thing he asked: how are the children? Not a word for me. Not a word about him either. We mean nothing to one another anymore. I imagine that's what he was trying to say. A pig? I think I'm within my rights to call him that. Nothing but hello goodbye. As cold as that. Afraid I might get my claws into him? I didn't reply straight away. I didn't want to give him the satisfaction of getting his children's news at the click of a finger. I call, you answer. You tell me what I want to know. Vicious. His call was unbelievably vicious, in spite of the soft voice he was putting on. He sounded slurred, and there was an unpleasant tone to his voice. Slippery, ugly, dirty. You couldn't pin the slightest question on that voice. I didn't recognise him. I told him so. "Roland, I don't recognise you." Did I even say his name? I don't recognise you. I must have done. I had his name stuck in my throat. What was going on with him? It was past ten o'clock. I wondered if he might be drunk.'

At Saint-Maur, two scruffy-looking buskers got on and began playing an old tune on the accordion. *Mais il est bien court, le temps des cerises. Pendants de corail qu'on cueille en rêvant.* 'Once, no more. One single phone call in two weeks. "How are the children?" If it wasn't for Élisabeth, I would have gone straight to the lawyer (or as she would have it, the thief). "Instructing the same lawyer as your husband. You must be mad." She speaks from experience. She was divorced herself last year. A no-fault settlement. She's still kicking herself about that.'

République. The crowd surged in both directions, bringing a new crush of people onto the train. The passengers rushing to board were preventing the others from getting off. The two musicians were carried off like leaves on the wind. *Mais il est bien court, le temps des cerises. Où l'on s'en va deux cueiller en rêvant.* 'After the phone call, not a peep. Where are you? How many times I asked myself the same question. What are you doing? If it wasn't for Samy, I might have thought he was dead. "Madame Desfeuillères? Samy Bouallem here." Soon I found myself waiting for his call.'

Arts-et-Métiers. 'Change at the next station. And Ludivine in tears every night. As soon as she gets home from school she starts crying. Unsettled, worried, instinctively understanding it all. "Papa's never coming back," she blurted out one evening. "He doesn't love us anymore." I had a lump in my throat. Corentin played the smart alec. "Why don't we just go to London to see papa?" Every night the same merry-go-round at the table with one too few place settings. For the first few days I carried on putting out a plate for him.'

Juliette was staring into space when the train stopped at Réaumur-Sébastopol. As the warning sound signalled the doors were about to close, she leapt from her seat, crashing into several of her fellow passengers as she left the carriage in the nick of time. 'Sorry.'

Standing on the platform she suddenly felt lost and had to fight the urge to turn back. 'Where am I going?' The first time she had been to meet Samy Bouallem, it had seemed like the right thing to do. He was, after all, her husband's colleague. Afterwards, Samy had continued to call her regularly to update her on the latest news from London. 'Everything's fine,' he would insist, trying to sound reassuring. He probably wouldn't have much more to tell her tonight. And yet Juliette wanted to see him. 'It'll be good to talk,' she told herself, putting her phone back in her bag, having had it ready to call Samy to cancel. Feeling more positive, she looked at her watch. 'I'm going to be late.' She raced towards the line 4 platform, holding herself back from running. The train was just pulling in. Clack. The doors closed behind her. 'I'll be at Montparnasse in less than fifteen minutes. He won't go through with it. How many times have I told myself? He'll backtrack, make a U-turn, Roland will come back. I've been back over the past. Our past. Every night I've dried my tears and tried to search for signs of what was coming. There must have been something. It just doesn't make sense otherwise. On the phone, when I finally worked up to asking him what was going on, he hung up. Maybe it was that night. Coming home later, grabbing hold of me as if I was an object, something he owned. Violent. I dropped my book. What was he trying to do? Or perhaps it was that time last summer. He pushed me away. Not now. Too tired. His head was spinning, so he said, but we had hardly drunk anything. I suppose he just didn't fancy me anymore. When we made love, it wasn't very good. No hiding from it. I tried to though. How could I be so stupid? The bastard.'

At Châtelet the train emptied out, unleashing a large crowd onto the platform, none of whom could see where they were going. Someone swore. A man and a woman were having an argument. The raised voices made Juliette jump. The train moved off again within seconds. 'I didn't really want to either. Why did we keep lying to one another? Roland had put on weight, basically let himself go. There was something about the man I had loved that was beginning to put me off him. His tone of voice had changed. At the beginning, his voice had made my spine tingle. Now when I hear it, his words slip over my skin like rain against a windowpane.'

Odéon. 'On Thursday I signed the divorce papers without a second thought. If someone had told me that two weeks ago, I wouldn't have believed them.' Saint-Sulpice. 'Done and dusted. Life goes on. I don't know who I am any more. The lawyer, Maître Candenœuvre, assured me that all the fault would lie with him.'

At Saint-Placide station Juliette took a mirror out of her bag. When she came up from the metro at Montparnasse, she took a deep breath of fresh air. The first autumnal evenings, the days getting shorter. As she walked, she repeated the line by Apollinaire of which she was so fond. *Mon Automne éternelle ô ma saison mentale*. Samy was waiting for her outside the restaurant.

'I think he's losing his mind,' he concluded as he and Juliette finished their starters. He had spoken to the lieutenant by phone the previous day. 'I hardly recognise him,' he added.

'Me neither,' agreed Juliette. 'Roland's a changed man.'

What else could they say? They changed the subject. The warm autumn evening made their thoughts turn to life's pleasures. Juliette used to love to dance. At the end of the meal Samy offered to take her to a nightclub.

'What, now?'

'Why not?'

She let him lead the way. Midway through the first dance Juliette knew she was coming back to life.

*

During the previous day's phone conversation, Lieutenant Desfeuillères hadn't given a full account of his research to his deputy. It was true he had gone to Barclays on the Friday morning, and had had no trouble getting the information he needed. Ranesh had done his job. As the lieutenant told Samy, John Burny had been living beyond his means. The guy was riddled with debt. So how had the victim come to have three thousand pounds cash in his pocket? The lieutenant was following up the theory of dirty money, as he told his deputy, who remained unconvinced. It seemed to him that his superior was jumping to the wrong conclusions, and he told him so.

'You're wasting your time in London.'

The conversation came to an abrupt end. Meanwhile John's bank accounts had turned up plenty of other things which the lieutenant had chosen to keep to himself.

A bank statement is like a road map. It allows you to find your bearings within the account holder's existence down to the nearest penny. John's credit card statements showed exactly when and where his card had been used. They could be used to build a day-by-day, minute-by-minute timetable of his movements. After three hours' work and a great many phone calls to locate the source of the transactions, the picture was becoming much clearer. During the week, from Monday to Thursday,

John barely left his local area. Most of the restaurants he ate at regularly were in Pimlico. John usually had lunch with someone else, judging by the size of the bill and the type of establishment: this was a meal for two. These transactions took place every other day. Roland concluded from this that the lunch companions took it in turns to pay. The other diner could only be Kate. In the evenings, from Monday to Wednesday at least, John ate alone and often in the same place, at a trattoria Roland had spotted while wandering round the area. There were a few anomalies of course, like the Tuesday night dinner at the Dorchester when the bill had come to four hundred pounds. Or the transaction at a pub in Elephant and Castle on a Wednesday: ninety-five pounds. Looked at over the course of a year, however, John's life during the week followed a fairly regular pattern. From Thursday night onwards, on the other hand, John's expenditure was all over the place, as was he himself. Some weekends, the credit card bills could add up to two thousand pounds. The average spend, in so far as it was possible to ascertain one, was in the region of a thousand. Most of the payments were made in bars, pubs and a few Soho nightclubs John visited assiduously of a Friday and Saturday. On some Saturdays, however, Roland traced John to south-east London, Shoreditch or even Brighton (with the hotel bill to show for it). In each case, establishing the time of John's last card payment gave a rough indication of what time he had headed home for the night; around 5 a.m. as a rule. Burny's life certainly wasn't boring.

The lieutenant was daydreaming. He was discovering London vicariously. He was following John on his nights out, which he imagined were pretty wild. By this point Roland had forgotten what he was in London for, and why he was looking into the accounts and the very existence of a man he had known nothing about two weeks previously. John had become familiar now. He thought about him non-stop, more about his life than his tragic end. Solving the crime itself was becoming an ever smaller part of his investigations, which now focused on the way John had gone about his business. 'He was more successful than I am,' thought the lieutenant. His life didn't stand up very well in comparison to John's. Roland had the feeling the best years of his life had been stolen from him. Juliette had given him two beautiful children, of course, but at the same rate as the kids grew, he saw himself decline. In the end it would be his children who would shovel the earth on top of his coffin. Hadn't they already begun to bury him? John was riddled with debts though, Roland tried to console himself. You ended up paying for everything one way or another, and John had paid the ultimate price.

Roland was clutching a bundle of statements covering the period from January to September. Each month John went further into the red, without the bank doing anything to stop him. On the contrary, in a letter dated

25 June they were offering to extend his credit limit. With debts racking up to one hundred thousand pounds, John should surely have had his card taken off him. Intrigued, Roland asked to see the statements for the five previous years. It took him less than a quarter of an hour to clear up the mystery of John's accounts. Every now and again a huge sum of money would appear in his account at just the right moment to pay off his debts. The money came from none other than the estate agency where Burny worked and these substantial injections of cash (thirty thousand pounds on 22 December 2007, for example) must correspond with commission earned on the sale of properties. These payouts had been top-dollar until the financial crisis came along and put an end to the golden age of bonuses. And so John had known exactly what he was doing when he went out spending a fortune on meals and holidays. His monthly budget, which had at first seemed suicidally out of control, now appeared to be perfectly well thought out. So there was no dirty money after all, no mafia connection or stolen artworks or illegal trade in drugs, weapons or people-smuggling; only a pleasure-seeker who, even when spending what might appear to the man on the street to be colossal sums of money, had accounted for every last pound. Everything was beginning to make sense, except, perhaps, the most important thing; that is, why John Burny had been murdered. Roland looked at his watch. It was just past one o'clock. If he hurried, he

could still catch Kate at work. He wanted to take her out for lunch. 'Just like John used to do!' he chuckled to himself.

'Closed' read the sign on the door of Dreams of Chelsea. Kate had already gone out for lunch. Roland stood there for a moment, wondering what to do. He didn't feel like eating by himself. Suddenly it occurred to him he had seen the information he needed on John's statement. If the truth was written in the cards, he knew exactly where to find Kate.

It was a pleasant spot, halfway between a restaurant and a cafe. The menu was mostly made up of salads and sandwiches. Sitting at the back of the small room, Kate was picking at a few cubes of cheese on a pile of lettuce and flicking through a magazine with an air of boredom.

'Hello!'

She looked up, more surprised than pleased to see the lieutenant. She remarked what a coincidence it was that he had chosen this restaurant among so many others in the area. She always came here for lunch, she said, without elaborating. She seemed to have nothing else to add. She stared at the lieutenant, who had just invited himself to join her without a by your leave. He had already begun studying the menu when she asked frostily, 'May I help you?'

Kate was putting him firmly in his place. Roland put

the menu down and looked her over. She had applied her make-up cleverly to mask her drawn features.

'Tired?' he asked warmly, evoking the intimacy their two bodies had shared three days before.

Kate glared back at him before leaning in to whisper what he had in any case just understood. 'It was just a good fuck!'

That morning, Roland had picked up the keys to John's apartment from his hotel reception, where Ranesh had had them dropped off. Roland had stuffed them into his jacket pocket without much thought. It was shaping up to be a busy day. Searching John Burny's apartment was just another thing to add to the list.

Yet as he pushed open the lacquered wooden door of the house on Moreton Place, Roland got a buzz of excitement. He was going into John's home. Normally the lieutenant brought another officer with him to carry out a search. If necessary, he would call a forensics team too. In those circumstances, surrounded by all those people, there was no room for any kind of emotional response. Desfeuillères was not entering someone's home; he was inspecting rooms, checking every nook and cranny. The person who had died was lost in the search for clues; lost for a second time. But today Roland was alone. He hadn't thought to take a pair of gloves. Ranesh hadn't offered him any help, and he hadn't asked for any. He was visiting John's house the way you visit a friend, or perhaps not like that at all. He wasn't sure. Like a thief, maybe.

The front door opened onto a hallway from which a stairway led to the floors above. On the ground floor, tucked off to the right, was John's flat. The key turned easily in the lock. 'There we go!' thought Roland. The front door creaked open. The wood had warped in the rain. The lieutenant crept in like a burglar, listening out for noises. It seemed there was no one home. No voices could be heard from the floors above. Roland tiptoed into the flat, having carefully closed the door behind him. 'I'm in,' he repeated to himself. Using the back of his sleeve, he wiped a few beads of sweat off his brow. It was muggy; a storm was brewing.

Nothing out of place, he noted, casting his eyes around the vast living room he had just entered. Everything appeared to be as John had left it when he closed the door of his flat on Friday 19 September, unaware that it would be for the last time. A slightly musty, stale smell hung in the air, giving everything a heavy, illusory quality. The curtains were drawn. Roland knew he was the first person to enter the flat since John's departure. According to Ranesh, the British police had decided not to visit the victim's address once they knew the investigation was being handled by the French. For a split second Roland saw John's body as it had taunted him at the morgue. So this was where John lived, or rather had lived. And that life had been very different from the lieutenant's. 'I could have lived another life too,' he told himself. He suddenly felt very alone, a stranger to his own existence and unable to identify with John's, even though he was standing in the very place where it had been played out.

Where to begin? Roland went to open the curtain, but had a change of heart. Someone might see him from the street. John seemed to have been a familiar face among his neighbours. A friend or passer-by like the crazy old woman he had encountered on his first visit to Moreton Place might judge his presence suspicious. They might call the police. Caught red-handed. He would have to explain himself. Call Ranesh? He would already have gone home for the weekend. Roland let his hand drop, brushing the length of the curtain. The sun was coming through the fabric, filling the room with a subdued light.

The living room was done up in a modern and tasteful style, as far as the lieutenant could tell, being no expert in such things. There wasn't much to say about the furniture. Yet he was surprised by how impersonal the decor was. It was so like the sets you might see in films or magazines that the room felt immediately familiar. It put you straight at ease, like a hotel lobby designed to be pleasant, functional and stylish, and to appeal to everyone. Roland was gradually beginning to relax. He left the living room to have a look round the other rooms. The apartment was spacious, with a well-equipped kitchen opening out onto a patio and, further down the corridor, two very nice bedrooms with a bathroom between them. Roland went from one room to another like a potential buyer trying to gauge the value of the property. The first impressions were good. You could definitely see yourself living here. Now to move on to the finer details.

Roland began with the bedroom that John must have slept in; the sheets were ruffled. At the foot of the bed lay four polo shirts in a range of colours, along with a pair of jeans John must have decided to leave behind. He had probably left in a hurry. Roland imagined Burny rushing home from work to quickly grab his things, taking a few seconds to choose between clothes before closing his suitcase and racing back out the door to catch his train. The corner of a laptop computer was sticking out from under the sheets. In spite of his haste, John must have very quickly checked his emails before leaving, a sign he may have been eagerly awaiting a response from someone. This could be the lead Roland needed to finally get his investigation moving.

He sat down on the bed to boot up the computer. The machine was already whirring into action when Roland felt overwhelmed with tiredness. Since his arrival in London the lieutenant had hardly had time to breathe. Everything was new to him. He lay back in spite of himself. The bed was soft. Roland couldn't stop himself falling straight into a deep sleep. The sound of thunder woke him two hours later. As he struggled to open his eyes, it took a moment to work out whose bed he had been sleeping in. What time was it? He didn't recognise the room. The room was in partial darkness, lit up every so often by streaks of lightning. A storm was raging across London. Roland blinked his eyes open. It was all coming back to him in waves. Lunch with Kate. The way she had blanked him. Three glasses of bad wine. Then he remembered how tired he was. Another flash of lightning lit up the room. John's room. Roland had needed that sleep, that's why he had dozed off so quickly. The rain began to pound against the French windows. He rubbed his eyes. He still didn't know what to make of anything. He felt like a passenger stepping off a sea crossing. The joy of being back on dry land, the sensation the body retains of still swaying. Was it down to the wine or the heat? Roland was very thirsty. Without hesitation he made his way into the kitchen and dug out a bottle of sparkling mineral water. Seeing the coffee machine made him want a cup. A few moments later the lieutenant was sitting in one of the armchairs in the living room with his coffee in front of him on the attractive glass table. With childlike curiosity, he was leafing through a specialist magazine he had just found. The warm and fuzzy post-nap feeling was getting stronger as he began to find his feet in John's apartment. It was a nice place. There was a welcoming feel to it that made it hard to leave.

So why not stay here? Roland asked himself. He'd be a hundred times better off here than in a hotel. There was no need to bring it up with Ranesh. A wide smile opened up on the lieutenant's face. He was relaxed, he felt comfortable in his own skin, he already felt at home here. He thanked God for London. The city was having a very positive effect on him. The 'I love London!' exhibition popped back into his mind. London really was a place of transformation.

The telephone rang. Who could be calling John two weeks after his death? Roland paused before picking up. It could easily be a wrong number. There was only one way to find out. Wasn't that why the lieutenant was here, to find things out? It was Kate at the other end of the line.

'I knew you'd still be there,' she said as soon as he answered.

Over lunch, Roland had told her he was planning to visit John's flat. She had replied with nothing more than a bored smile intended to make it abundantly clear that the lieutenant's case, and the lieutenant himself, had ceased to interest her. Her tone of voice was different now. There was more energy to it. She teasingly asked her one-time lover questions. Had he found the skeleton in the cupboard? Then she asked outright if he had looked at the pictures. Her voice was completely emotionless. Taken off guard, Roland thought best to lie, telling her he had only been able to look at them very quickly. Kate sounded disappointed. She had clearly been hoping for a different reaction.

'You're a funny one,' she said. 'Is that really all you have to say about them?' she pressed.

Which photos was she talking about? They must be compromising in some way. Illegal, possibly. The kind of pictures you weren't supposed to own. Something appalling, thought the lieutenant as he told Kate he had seen it all before.

'OK, OK,' she said, not wishing to seem easily shocked.

Sounding once again cheerful, almost affectionate, she went straight on to suggest she might pop round to his place – that is, John's place. She wanted to show him a couple of things he wasn't likely to find by himself. She knew John's flat very well.

'I've been round there so many times,' she said with sadness, as if she had suddenly remembered her old friend was dead.

An hour later she was standing outside the door with a smile on her lips and an irresistibly cheeky look on her face. She was carrying three bags bearing the emblem of a famous London department store. Roland welcomed her in as if he owned the place. It was almost five o'clock. Having barely made it through the door, Kate asked for a drink. She was gasping. It had been a tough day. After work, she had run down to Harvey Nichols to pick up a few things, including a Paul Smith shirt she thrust into Roland's arms:

'That's to help you forget the huff I was in at lunch time,' she said, putting on a look of contrition.

But within seconds she wore a new face again. With a mischievous grin, she added, 'And to make you forget the checked shirt you're wearing.'

While Roland was putting on his new shirt, one with a flowery design, Kate disappeared for a moment, coming back holding up a pair of jeans as though lifting a trophy. These were the spoils of war.

'John wore them all the time. They might be a bit tight on you, but they should just about fit.'

Roland stared back at Kate, speechless. He did up the last few buttons of the shirt, snorting at the red Armani label jeans.

'Please. Do it for me.'

Roland pretended to go along with it, despite how uncomfortable he felt at having to get changed while a woman stood looking at him. Having undone his belt, he looked up in search of encouragement.

'The problem is the stomach,' said Kate, examining Roland as if contemplating the purchase of a knick-knack of dubious quality. 'Turn around. Very good legs and bum. Nice strong shoulders. Height? Let me guess. Same as John, I reckon.'

'Six foot.'

'Knew it.'

Roland's embarrassment became more and more

palpable the longer Kate scrutinised him. The excitement he had initially felt as she circled around him was melting away like snow in the sun. She was right. Roland was the same height as John. He had noticed the same thing at first glance at the morgue.

'You could do with some exercise,' said Kate, who appeared to be seeing her lover's body for the first time. 'Why don't you go and work out at John's gym? It's just around the corner.'

Roland told her his investigation had already taken him there, much to Kate's approval.

'You're not wasting any time.'

'I'll put them on later,' he said, hanging the jeans over the back of one of the chairs. 'How about we talk about John now?'

'You know pretty much all there is to know, don't you?' asked Kate, taking a sip of gin and tonic. 'Wow. John's gin is out of this world. He used to get it shipped over from Minorca. He was over the top like that, John.'

'He had exactly the right idea,' Roland argued back.

'Have you looked at the pictures? I think they speak for themselves. What more can I say?' said Kate, stony-faced. 'Pass me a cigarette.'

'You could tell me who he hung out with. If he had anything on his mind. Were you aware of the state of his finances?'

'You mean his credit cards? I owe twice as much as him!' she said, taking a long puff of smoke.

'No enemies?' Roland pressed on, lighting a cigarette for himself.

'He had enemies all over the place! Half of Soho had it in for him, and for good reason: John was a complete slut!' she said, rolling her eyes. 'Every night he promised them the stars. The next morning he was gone, as he used to delight in telling me.'

'Might one of these guys have wanted him dead?'

'All of them! But none of them did it,' she said, suddenly serious and almost confrontational.

'How can you be sure?' asked Roland, surprised at her vehemence.

'It's patently obvious,' she shot back. 'You want to know what I think? I think John was just in the wrong place at the wrong time. He found himself in the path of a nutcase. The world's full of crazy people. You should know.'

The lieutenant called the game off. He wasn't going to get anything out of Kate, and she seemed to have stopped listening anyway. Sitting on the sofa, she was staring at her lieutenant with the same greedy expression he had caught on her face the moment he had handcuffed her.

'You know,' she said after a brief silence when she appeared to collect her thoughts, 'You know you're a fucking good fuck!'

What could Desfeuillères say to that? Could he go one step further? Maybe, he told himself, already getting excited but lost for words. He made to stand up, but she held him back.

'Not now. Next week.'

She was holding a reception that evening. She had to go home to get changed. It was important that she made the right impression. She couldn't go greeting her guests with cuff marks on her wrists.

'Go one further, that's right,' thought Roland. 'You fuck like a whore.' As if she could read his thoughts, she suggested he join her on a flat viewing the following Tuesday. He could get a feel for John's work 'on the job'.

'But how long are you actually staying in London for?' she finally asked.

Her question brought the lieutenant back to reality. The light was fading in the living room. Time was ticking on. Roland checked his watch, suddenly feeling anxious. He had promised the prosecutor he would ring him at the end of the day to give an update on the progress of his inquiries.

The prosecutor, Jean de Loustal, was indeed waiting for his call, and there was a note of annoyance in his voice as he picked up the phone. If it was six o'clock in London that meant seven o'clock in Paris, he jokingly reminded the lieutenant. It was Friday. The prosecutor was off to the Opéra Bastille for the evening.

'Janácek's *The Cunning Little Vixen*. Do you know it? It's supposed to be very good. I'm told it's a very good production.'

Then, without leaving Roland the chance to respond, he asked for a round-up of the investigation.

'Where are you at with it? I'm in a hurry. Just give me the important bits.'

Roland's words came out in a muddle. He didn't know how to present the facts. The prosecutor lost his temper.

'You've got nothing! You're wasting your time in London. Get on the first train back to Paris. I'll try to bat the case back to the Brits.'

Roland began to protest. He had a lead. Unfortunately it was quite complicated to explain.

'Give me another week.'

'Alright,' Jean de Loustal replied grudgingly. 'Luckily for you, I have to go out now. One week, and that's it.'

Then he hung up.

Kate had disappeared off to the kitchen, from where Roland could hear her tidying up. After the news of the murder, she had warned the cleaning lady not to touch anything. She thought the police might search the flat for clues. In the meantime the water, phone, gas and electricity had been left connected, she explained to Roland, who had just joined her. It wasn't until several days after John's death that she got a call from a detective with an unpronounceable name.

'And what did he say?' asked Roland, intrigued.

'He just asked me to leave everything as it was. He said the investigation was moving forward and they'd keep me up-to-date.'

'What about John's parents?'

'They died more than ten years ago.'

'Brothers and sisters?'

'Only child.'

John's life was closing in on itself like a mollusc that shuts when you touch it. His death had not brought any revelation, cast any light at all on his life. John appeared to have expressed the full contents of his heart while he was alive. A charming guy, a son of a bitch, at the end of the day he was all of those things. There was no mystery about him. Roland was gradually coming to see that investigating John's life was an act of madness. He would get no answers, because the questions were pointless. In a way, Kate was right. Whether you died naturally, by accident or by strangulation, death would always remain unfathomable and absurd. Incidentally, Kate appeared to have already forgotten John. She had probably deleted his name from her contacts list minutes after hearing the news.

'The storm's over,' she said, leading Roland back into the living room. The sun was going down. All the flat had to show for itself now were hazy, gloomy shadows. Kate flung open the curtains in one sweeping movement, the act of a person used to unveiling hidden dwellings to curious eyes.

'We're going to put the flat on the market,' she said in a voice that chimed perfectly with her gesture. 'The lawyer dealing with the will asked us to sort it out.'

Then, turning to face Roland, she looked him straight in the eye and asked if he'd like to move into John's place. The flat was now in the hands of the estate agency. No one would have any objections. He affected a moment's hesitation.

'You'll be better off here than in a hotel,' Kate said to convince him.

Soon afterwards she left Roland alone. He fell back onto the sofa. It was an attractive fabric-covered settee strewn with plump, soft cushions. Desfeuillères spread his arms along the back of the sofa and stretched out his legs, casting his eyes around him. It was no longer the piercing gaze of an inspector leading an inquiry that ran over the furniture, but that of a man moving house. So now this was home. A flatscreen TV was mounted on the wall opposite him. Roland picked up the remote lying on the coffee table and turned it on. The daily happenings of the world via the news channel brought some life back to the living room. Normality was returning to John's home, or rather Roland's home. The faceless voiceover's measured tone was reassuring. Roland stood up to make himself another drink. In the kitchen, he noticed that Kate had emptied the fridge. A half-full bin stood in the way of the patio door. Roland tied the bag and took it outside to tidy the place up. He was settling in. He began to write the next day's shopping list on a notepad which must have been placed there for that very purpose.

With his gin and tonic in one hand, he started opening the cupboards and drawers. There was everything he needed here, plus a whole lot more. The flat was over-equipped. Still holding his glass, he went from room to room feeling a mixture of curiosity and amusement, happy to be discovering his new surroundings. And he really couldn't find fault; it was just lovely. Roland finally stopped in front of the wardrobe in John's room. Inside were two horizontal rails. Several suits and a few pairs of trousers, mostly jeans, were stored on one side, while fifty-odd shirts hung on the other. Roland trailed his hand over the fabrics. The luxury of the outfits was palpable. Further down, the boxers and socks had been neatly folded away. One of the drawers caught his attention; it contained nothing but a shirt which John had put away still in its wrapping. It was a very nice midnight blue shirt, probably designer. Roland took it out of its drawer and began pulling off the packaging. It looked about the right size. The neck was a half-size bigger than the rest of John's shirts. He must have bought it by mistake and put it away until he got round to taking it back. Roland took it to be a kind of welcome gift from destiny. He quickly put the shirt on, noting it fitted like a glove, then put away the one Kate had just given him, judging it to be too out-there. The same went for the red jeans she had tried to get him to try on. On the other hand, the black jeans dangling from a hanger, which he had glimpsed as he caught his reflection in the mirror inside the wardrobe, now he really did like those. Moments later Roland was standing admiring the new him, transformed from top to bottom. Dressed like John, he felt like a different man. All he had had to do was suck his stomach in a bit.

Night had fallen and the glass of gin and tonic Roland had carried from room to room was now empty. On John's bed, a weak light blinked intermittently from the laptop Desfeuillères had turned on when he arrived. It was like a fine stream of breath clinging on to life, as though it were John lying in the darkness, waiting to be revived. With one click, the machine was woken up. Next the inbox was flagging more than a hundred emails. At the top of the screen, the clock read seven o'clock already. The afternoon had gone too quickly. There were still several things Roland needed to sort out. He returned to the living room where the television was still droning on, showing the day's news on a loop. In Paris, a hold-up on the Champs-Élysées had left three people dead.

Right, thought Roland: 1) go back to the hotel to collect my things and check out; 2) give Samy a ring; 3) call David; 4) search John's flat. Actually, no. There'll be plenty of time for that tomorrow.

Three-quarters of an hour later, Roland was back home. He had thought it best to call Samy from his hotel room, putting off telling him about his change of address until Monday. The conversation had been short and bad-tempered. The questions Samy asked had wound Roland up, while the younger man had been annoyed at his superior's tone.

Now it was time to give David a ring. He was glad to sweep the previous phone call from his mind. It was Friday, going-out night. Roland had kept a mental note of some of the places John hung out at weekends. If he suggested meeting up with David in one of these bars, he could kill two birds with one stone. It was high time he got down on the ground to kick-start his inquiry. David picked up at the first ring but didn't recognise Roland to begin with, taking him for someone else, though without appearing to know exactly who that someone else might be. The questions he asked – where, when and how – made Roland laugh. David clearly didn't live a very orderly life. He must meet so many people that it was impossible for him to remember who he had had a drink with the night before. Roland ended up spelling out that he had been a friend of John Burny's.

'That's why I'm calling you,' he said slightly awkwardly.

It clicked straight away; David remembered who he was and suggested the two of them should meet.

'I was going to suggest the same thing.'

'Tonight?' ventured David, a slight note of uncertainty in his voice.

It was agreed they would meet that same evening at 10 p.m. at the Duke of Edinburgh. Roland had picked this pub at random from the three places he knew of in Soho. Luck had been on his side judging by David's reaction; he seemed delighted to have the chance to go back to a pub he hadn't visited for two whole weeks, practically an eternity.

The rain had started falling again. It no longer came down in squalls, but a light drizzle that made the surface of the road shimmer under the streetlights. Roland closed the living room window which Kate had left wide open. He shivered. The first autumn chills were on their way. The lieutenant instinctively rubbed his shoulders. The jacket he had brought with him from Paris was no longer adequate. He returned to John's wardrobe and put on a jumper which had caught his eye earlier. Then it occurred to him to check not John's emails, but his own. He hadn't looked at them for two days. Turning the computer back on, he was faced with the hundred emails John had received which he was yet to read. 'They can wait,' he told himself as he closed the window with a click of the mouse. He typed in the address of his email server to find fifteen or so messages waiting for him, including two from his lawyer and one from Maître Candenœuvre. Juliette's lawyer was writing to inform him that his wife had signed the divorce papers. The other messages were mostly just spam, which Roland deleted without reading. He had barely closed the lid of the computer when he felt a pang of hunger in his stomach. He could go through John's correspondence tomorrow as part of his search of the flat. But was there really any point in going ahead with that, now he had moved in? In any case, if he wanted to make it to his meeting on time, taking account of how long the Tube journey would take, he really must find somewhere to eat now. He remembered the trattoria that John seemed to have treated as his daily canteen. There were a great many dishes to choose from. He could just fancy a plate of cured meats or a bowl of pasta.

'I'll have spaghetti alle vongole,' he said to himself as he rushed out the door.

7

Lieutenant Desfeuillères was leaning on the bar at the Duke of Edinburgh, waiting for his pint of Guinness as the sweat dripped off him. The pub was packed, just as it had been the previous Friday. An oddball crowd spilled out onto the pavement, turning the road into a meat market. Punters seemed to invite passers-by to take their fancy. Roland asked himself why he had come back to the Duke, shortening the name as David had done repeatedly a week earlier. Was it the wish to wind down with a drink, or to see Soho one last time? He was heading back to Paris on Sunday. Next to him, two guys in their thirties were all over one another as they waited for their drinks. Coming up for air, the drunker of the two gave Roland a wink; he turned away.

He paid for the drink that had just been handed to him by the athletic-looking barman with glistening bare chest. After taking a swig of Guinness, Roland tried to beat a path across the room to find a quieter spot. A strong stench of stale beer and sweat hung in the air. A group of five Brazilians took up the middle of the room, causing much amusement. It was a motley gathering of differing ages, skin colours and clothing selections. The youngest of the group, a short, muscular mixed race man, was wearing a pair of skinny jeans designed to show off unlikely-looking bulges. His open shirt revealed a smooth, hairless chest which shone as if it had been polished. Nature had not been so kind to the man next to him, a thirty-something gangly beanpole more conservatively attired. He hid his scrawny frame under baggy cotton trousers and a designer polo shirt. There was a look of anxiety on his skinny face, which he tried to distract from with a nervous tic of opening and closing the Louis Vuitton bag which hung over his shoulder. The other three were over fifty, one white, one black, one Asian. They had dressed up in garish colours which stood out in this pub where blue jeans and white T-shirts were the norm. They spoke at the tops of their voices, hardly pausing for breath, all the while eyeing up a crowd impervious to their hungry stares. Roland was trying to get past when one of them called out to him in broken English, saying words to the effect that he might like to follow him into the toilets. The lieutenant pretended not to hear. He would have walked straight past them if the little olive-skinned muscle man hadn't grabbed him by the arm and pulled him up against him, in a move intended to be both forceful and seductive. Without giving his victim the chance to fight back, he had his lips all over Roland's neck as he whispered promises of eternal love, followed by a more direct 'Fuck me'. Almost immediately he let go of him again, like a child which has gone off its toy. Roland seized his chance to escape via the exit, which was being diligently guarded by a humungous bouncer. The party continued on the other side of the door. At least twenty punters were crammed onto the pavement with drinks in hand, shirts rumpled, already pissed. Having elbowed his way through, Roland managed to find a gap between two groups of men each with their backs turned to him. The full moon made the street bizarrely bright.

The lieutenant finished his Guinness, glancing anxiously this way and that, asking himself once again what he was doing back in this part of town when his investigation had just been shelved on the prosecutor's orders. This was now the third time he had hung out around here since he had met David the Friday before. In the meantime, he had tried some other pubs, some of them rather more appealing than this one. You even came across one or two women in them. Yet it was to the Duke of Edinburgh that he had returned tonight for the sole reason — he now accepted, as he knocked back the rest of his pint — that this pub had been John's rallying point, as David had explained. If you were looking for John, he had told Roland, you knew sooner or later you'd find him propping up the bar at the Duke. Roland looked down into his empty glass. He was in two minds whether to leave. What did he think he was going to find here? Yet he had no desire to go home. The pub would be closing in less than half an hour. The bell would ring for last orders any moment now. 'Where am I going?' the lieutenant suddenly asked himself. He was no more keen to return to Paris. The truth was, he no longer had any idea what to do with himself. As he stared off into space, Roland's gaze fell on a young man standing on the opposite pavement, leaning back against the wall and apparently staring right back at him.

Actually, he was a very young man indeed, more like a boy, thought the lieutenant, before changing his mind. He must be older than he looked to be hanging around here. The guy knew Roland had seen him, but carried on eyeballing him regardless. With his hands in his pockets and his back against the wall, he looked like an alley cat waiting to pounce. Roland looked away, uncomfortable, and tried to appear unfazed, casting his eyes into his empty glass. By the time he looked up again, he was gone. Good-looking guy, Roland couldn't help thinking to himself. He felt vaguely unsettled. He slipped inside the pub to order a second pint of beer.

It had been a busy week, and it had ended on a piece of dramatic news. The story had only broken that morning but was already being beamed around the world. A murder had been committed aboard the Dover–Calais ferry. Roland hadn't stopped thinking about it all day.

And yet the week had started promisingly. On Monday, Ranesh had informed Roland that the train company was willing to provide the list of passengers on board the Express 0290. Roland headed straight for their head office, a stone's throw from St Paul's Cathedral, where he had been handed a bundle of a dozen or so pages on strict instructions not to share the information with any press organisation or commercial body. This was confidential data. The company's reputation was at stake, etc. etc. Roland had consented to all their demands, anxious to get home with the list from which he hoped the identity of the killer would miraculously emerge.

The cross-Channel train had a capacity of seven hundred and fifty passengers, but it wasn't full on the night of the murder. No doubt the time of day John was travelling explained why there were only five hundred and forty-eight people on board. Still a fair number of people, the lieutenant realised as he spread the list of names out on the coffee table.

He leaned back to take in the whole picture. The killer was there in front of him somewhere, hidden among the hundreds of names. Then he moved in closer. Perhaps he had the murderer under his finger, right there, he said to himself as he pointed to a name at random. Andrew McGuff, he read. How was he meant to know? Roland picked out another name, Pablo Lazare, then a third, Simon Notable, and a fourth, Claire Marivaud.

On another sheet, the names Sumudu Panesh, George Smith, Laurence Manin, Alfonso Di Leonardi and Ahmed al-Djazaïri appeared. Some of the surnames were hard to pronounce. They could be Korean or Chinese, perhaps. The whole world seemed to have come together on board that train. Identifying every passenger was going to be a monumental task. Each and every one of them would need to be contacted in order to verify who they were. But how was he going to track down this passenger, for example, a Mr Esquoril who might now be in Paris, or Lisbon, or why not Sydney? It seemed like mission impossible. Roland rang Ranesh to ask for help. He wanted a team of three or four people along with the same number of phone lines and internet connections. He went into great detail setting out his plan of attack while the inspector said nothing. The French lieutenant guessed that around two-thirds of the passengers would pick up the phone. It would take no time at all to verify their identities. The police forces of the countries concerned would be sure to lend them assistance. Then they could concentrate their efforts on those they had not managed to get hold of. It might take, say, two days to locate the first of these, another three to find the rest. By Friday, things should begin to look a bit clearer.

'After all,' said Roland, who had run out of arguments and was beginning to shuffle under the silence at the other end of the line, 'we know the murderer was on this train and he must have been travelling under some identity or other.'

'For free?' asked Ranesh. The case was in the hands of the French police. It was therefore out of the question for the UK to hand over a single one of its officers free of charge. 'I suggest you call Paris.'

Roland hung up, seething, and immediately tapped in Jean de Loustal's number. He was soon told where to go. Send two extra guys to London on a case that's going nowhere? You're having a laugh, lieutenant. The prosecutor put the phone down, though not before reminding Roland that he expected to see him in his office first thing on Monday.

The further the lieutenant got with his inquiry, the clearer it seemed to him that no one cared about John Burny's murder. But: 1) Could he really say he was making any progress whatsoever in this inquiry? 2) Wasn't the investigation doomed from the word go? 3) Why had he been allowed to come to London in the first place? Feeling disheartened, Roland drew one more name out of the hat. This time, it was Russian, a certain Dimitri Rasnikov. Who was hiding behind this surname? Was Dimitri really called Dimitri? This was ridiculous. Trying to find the identity of an unknown person most likely travelling under a false name was nigh on impossible. By association, Roland's thoughts turned back to John. Who was he? What exactly did Roland know about him? A charming man, a son of a bitch, and that was pretty much it. Over the weekend, the lieutenant had kept putting off going through the victim's emails. It had taken less than twenty-four hours for John's flat to feel familiar. Roland helped himself to food from John's cupboards, used John's kitchen, sat in John's chair. He was settling in to John's place; he wasn't going to search it. He had even given up on the idea of examining the photos Kate had mentioned, which had sounded potentially crucial to the inquiry. In one decisive move, the lieutenant swept the sheets of paper off the coffee table and into an envelope. The question was, if Roland didn't know who John Burny was, what could he say about himself?

When Roland turned round, the boy was right there behind him, almost touching him. Roland jumped, visibly taken aback. The guy he had taken for a rent boy had appeared again as if by magic, yet Roland's pleasant surprise at seeing him again was tinged with a strange, dull sense of unease that he couldn't make sense of: the kid scared him. The boy looked him straight in the eyes, before apologising:

'I thought you were someone else.'

He made as if to leave, but Roland held him back with the offer of a drink. A few moments later they were in a back room the young man had directed him to, away from prying eyes.

'We can talk more easily here,' he said as he led him

into the room, acting as if the pair of them went way back.

Roland was surprised to discover the existence of this small room, apparently known only to regulars. The crowd was beginning to thin out and the last few punters were gathered around the bar. Roland found himself alone in conversation with the boy, sitting on a beaten-up leather sofa that reeked of alcohol and sweat. He still couldn't get over his astonishment. It seemed to him that this guy could have taken him wherever he wanted. He would have followed him, no questions asked. For now, he was speechless. The boy spoke first. His name was Hassan and he said he was Afghan. His strongly accented English and sharp, rugged facial features appeared to support this statement, which the lieutenant was not in a position to verify. Hassan more or less fitted Roland's mental impression of what an Afghan looked like. In any case, it wasn't the time or the place to try to find out more. Roland in turn introduced himself as a French estate agent who had come to London looking to snap up some good deals. Property prices were in meltdown. Now was the time to buy. The conversation struggled to flow. Every time Roland spoke, Hassan stared at him in amazement; feeling increasingly self-conscious, Roland stumbled over every word. Without warning, the kid grabbed the lieutenant by the back of his jacket, pulling him close before he had the time or inclination to do anything about it; once again Roland found his instinctive reaction to be afraid being dulled by some form of desire.

'It's the jacket,' said Hassan, his eyes glued to the fabric. 'You're wearing the same jacket as the guy I confused you with. How funny!' he added, in an effort to sound casual.

Roland sat still. He was waiting. He could feel the young man's warm breath against his neck. He was waiting for him to spot the shirt and jeans. How would he react to the evidence of his imposture? Chance, thought Roland, most things can be put down to chance. John's jacket and shirt weren't so rare that no one else could have bought the same ones. He could easily share the same taste as the man the boy had taken him for. Roland was planning his next move, like a policeman in the presence of a murderer. In a matter of seconds, Hassan cried out again:

'You won't believe me.'

He seemed to be in a daze, staring off into space. He let go of the jacket and huddled into the far corner of the sofa, putting some distance between himself and Roland, who was still contemplating what to say or do. Who exactly was this Hassan anyway? Probably a rent boy John had picked up. The two of them might have gone out another three or four times, judging by Hassan's knowledge of his former lover's wardrobe. Or perhaps the boy had had a love affair with John, which would explain his melancholy disposition as he sat half-slumped on the sofa. Roland recalled what Kate had said about John. She had painted him as a son of a bitch. A charming man, yes, but a son of a bitch nonetheless, who disappeared the morning after when he'd got what he wanted. How could he have had a love affair? Roland was on the verge of telling the boy his true identity and the reason why he was in London, but he stopped himself. He might be onto something with this kid. He went with a half-lie, or a partial truth. Hiding his profession but revealing he had known John. Besides, was it really a lie to say he worked in property? Since the previous Tuesday he had been seriously considering quitting the police force to throw himself into selling flats, as Kate had suggested. It was last orders at the bar. Now was the time to act.

'Another drink?' asked Roland.

Hassan shook his head and made to stand up. Roland felt more slighted than he ought to have done. So the boy wasn't interested in him? He was seized with panic. He had to find a way to keep Hassan from leaving. 'I need to get more out of him,' he told himself, without quite convincing himself that was actually the reason. He just needed the kid to stay with him, that was all. 'He's the one I'm looking for, he finally told himself,' without being able to put his finger on what it was he was trying to find in the boy. Hassan stood up and began putting on his anorak. He gave Roland a nod as he prepared to leave. It was time for Roland to talk.

'I'm a friend of John's. Or was, rather. It's his jacket I'm wearing.'

Hassan stared at him in disbelief before sitting back down. He grasped the back of the jacket again and stroked the fabric.

'Nice jacket, isn't it?' he said. Roland was wondering if he'd done the right thing bringing John into it, when the young man asked him flatly, 'He's dead, isn't he?'

There was no trace of emotion on his face. He had let go of John's jacket and let his hand fall on Roland's thigh.

'Yes. An accident. Did you know him well?' the lieutenant ventured.

'Hardly at all,' replied Hassan.

After that, he fell quiet. He didn't move, except for his hand gently rubbing Roland's leg. He seemed determined to say nothing more on the subject. The lieutenant realised the only way forward was to throw a casual remark into the conversation or mention something that would take him back to an earlier time and get him talking in spite of himself. Roland didn't know exactly how he would go about it but he had the whole night ahead of him; Hassan seemed to have given up on the idea of leaving.

In the absence of any other ideas, he asked again 'One last drink?'

'OK,' came the reply.

When Roland returned with two pints of Guinness

between his hands and sat down beside the boy, he noticed a complete change in him. A broad smile ran from one side of his angular face to the other. He grabbed the glass Roland held out to him and drank half his pint in one go, before asking jovially if Roland planned to stay long in London.

'Two or three weeks. I'm not sure yet actually.'

Roland copied Hassan, downing his drink as if dying of thirst. This was his third Guinness and the alcohol was beginning to warm him up. He felt his confidence returning. He had the nerve to do whatever it took. So he told Hassan that the other reason he was in London was to sort out John's estate; they were old friends, he mentioned in passing.

'I'm staying in his flat,' he ended by saying, hoping to provoke a reaction.

But Hassan didn't pick up on the comment. He had just finished his drink. Visibly excited, he asked out of the blue, 'Where to now?'

A week earlier, Roland had been in the same pub, but with David. The first thing David remarked on finding the lieutenant leaning on the bar with a pint of Guinness in front of him was that he shared John's liking for Guinness. He, on the other hand, was not a big drinker, and ordered a Coke. The lieutenant seized on David's opening gambit to keep the conversation on John. What did he know about him? David dodged the question, instead placing his arm around Roland's shoulder and smiling adoringly at him. Evidently the man hadn't come here to talk about the past.

Roland had initially been taken aback, unsure of how to extricate himself from the tight spot he found himself in. David seemed to think it was a dead cert, so to bluntly knock him back seemed unkind. With a body like his, David probably wasn't used to encountering any resistance once he had his sights set on someone. And tonight he had gone all out. Recently showered, he had drenched himself in a pungent eau de toilette that could be detected ten yards away. Glued to Roland's side, with his arm still draped over his shoulder, he carried on smiling the same saccharine smile that made him look like an imbecile.

'I just love the French,' he finally said, after appearing to spend a great deal of time gathering his thoughts.

That's when Roland made up his mind to reveal his true identity and the reasons why he was in London.

'I'd like to ask you a few questions,' he said, wriggling free of his seducer's grip.

Lover boy stepped back in shock. He had been expecting Roland to say something altogether different. Yet once he had recovered from that bombshell, David leaned in again to ask the lieutenant a question. He was quite happy to talk about John, but first he wanted to know if Roland was gay. Roland sensed he was better off not letting the man down.

'Of course,' he replied, smiling suggestively as David had done.

And to add weight to this assertion, he added that that was the reason he had taken on the case. John's death had touched him. 'It touches us all,' he added emphatically. David couldn't help but agree, placing his hand on the Frenchman's shoulder once more.

'It's a good thing there are people like you in the police,' he said.

To be honest, he went on to admit, John's death hadn't come as all that much of a surprise. John was a bit of a bastard who had left a trail of casualties in his wake. David was one of them. He then began to talk about his own life, not so much describing John as the consequences of John walking out on him.

'I loved him so much,' he confessed.

David had planned to spend his life with John Burny. Everything was going so well. He had even begun looking for a flat for them both. David loved Chelsea, as did John. They were made for one another. Yet John had changed overnight. David had walked into the Duke of Edinburgh one evening and found John in the arms of another man. The son of a bitch! And in spite of the perfect smile that was permanently fixed on his face, David swore he had never got over it. What else could he say about John? Since the pub was about to close, David dragged Roland on a tour around Soho. Several times he put his arm around his new friend's shoulder, only to whip it away again, unsure of himself, no doubt intimidated to be walking alongside a cop. Eventually, at around two in the morning, having taken Roland to a night club, the handsome athlete had made a move on a rather fat, repulsive-looking man, disappearing after him without a word of goodbye.

'Where to now?' asked Hassan again.

'To the Paradise!' replied Roland.

The lieutenant could see the situation was getting out of hand. He was now playing a whole new ball game, whose rules he didn't understand. He didn't feel an ounce of regret. Just that same vague feeling of unease he had been plagued with on and off since he had first spotted Hassan, which was still gnawing away at him. In Roland's eyes, this was another reason not to analyse things too much. He should just charge right in. 'Where am I going?'

'To the Paradise!' he repeated to the cab driver.

The Paradise was a night club David had told him about. John used to spend an hour or two there every Saturday; just long enough to snare his next prey. The cab was making its way down Charing Cross Road towards the Thames. Sitting either side of the back seat, Hassan and Roland watched the streets of London passing before their eyes. Neither said a word. Roland wondered what Hassan was thinking about. Was he remembering one of his nights out with John? Having reached the Houses of Parliament, the driver took a left along the river. A few moments later he let out his two passengers in a dirty, poorly lit alleyway a hundred yards from the entrance to the Paradise. Clubgoers were being subjected to a thorough search on the door, causing a long queue to form and spill into the road. First you had to empty your pockets, then go through a security scanner before finally showing a piece of ID. No one seemed to mind having to put up with this police-style exercise, which was overseen by two burly bouncers. Roland looked nervously at Hassan. He didn't believe a word of the sketchy details the guy had told him about his background. The fear in the boy's eyes at the sight of the police officers patrolling Soho had left the lieutenant in little doubt: Hassan was not above board. But just as they reached the front of the queue, he produced a student card which seemed to do the trick. The bouncer let him in without a second look.

Inside the club, a dense crowd of people stood in their way. Under the Gothic arches of the vast room, several podiums had been erected on which go-go dancers were enthusiastically shaking their stuff. These superb creatures contorted themselves to the relentless beat of the deafening music, striking a succession of raunchy poses like mechanical dolls. At their feet, young bare-chested bodies rubbed against one another, compelled to keep moving as though it was impossible for them to stop. Hassan and Roland stood open-mouthed by the door, hesitant, not yet part of the party in full swing before them. The young man seemed enthralled, while Roland felt out of place here, where the average age must be under twenty-five. He thought about turning around and leaving. But where to? It was too late to turn back now. The lieutenant got up on tiptoe to survey the room, which seemed to him like an enormous cage filled with wild animals. The club functioned like a well-oiled machine; the cogs picked you up as you hit the dance floor and dropped you back down again in the early hours of the morning, knackered and in pieces. The lieutenant started to edge back, but Hassan put his arm around his waist and led him into the crowd.

The machine took care of the rest. You just had to let yourself be swept along by the tight mass of clubbers, and before you knew it you were dancing. Crushed from all sides, Roland soon found himself squashed up against this kid he had known for barely two hours. He felt the boy's slim, almost skinny, wiry frame moulding into his sagging adult body. They had been dancing for less than five minutes when Hassan grabbed the lieutenant's neck, pulled his face towards him and kissed him full on the mouth. A moment later, a shift in the beat of the music caused a wave of movement across the crowd, separating them from one another. Still reeling, Roland found himself face to face with a new partner almost as attractive and barely older than Hassan, who was equally keen to dance and to impress. His golden skin was shiny with sweat. He wore the same flat, vacant smile that had struck Roland when he had seen it on David's face. The lieutenant looked away, trying to find Hassan, but he had disappeared, swallowed up by the crowd. Roland felt a rush of panic. He was afraid he might have lost him. Maybe he had already gone off with someone else. The dream came to an abrupt end. He stopped dancing in order to escape the hypnotic frenzy brought about by the metallic, repetitive beat. Standing still, Roland found himself fighting the current, tossed about, thrust from side to side. He searched in vain for any sign of Hassan's slight frame. He was surrounded by a sea of identical ecstatic faces, bare, muscular shoulders and chests dripping with sweat. Hassan had vanished into thin air. Roland suddenly felt alone and out of place in these ridiculous pseudo-bacchanalian surroundings. Next to him, a rather frightening-looking hairy red-headed giant was gleefully popping pills. Further away, a wheezing, puce-faced older guy was snorting white powder. On his own, Roland felt lost. He felt an intense, urgent need to kiss the boy again; he still had the taste of him on his lips. As he turned away to avoid the ginger giant, he bumped into Hassan. For a moment they simply stared at one another. The kid seemed surprised to see Roland again. Roland took matters into his own hands, grabbing Hassan and kissing him roughly. The boy didn't put up a fight, but let his whole body fall into the arms of the lieutenant.

*

They had spoken on the phone several more times. After every call, Samy said he no longer understood his superior. Juliette on the other hand had given up hope of hearing from the man who was still her husband, for now at least. These days she instead looked forward to the almost daily call from Samy; she enjoyed listening to him talk about himself, about her, and even sometimes about the two of them together. This Friday night she had invited him round for dinner. The children had been sent to their grandparents' for the weekend. Juliette felt the need to put her stamp on the apartment she had shared with Roland for so many years. She had already moved a few items of furniture around. She was thinking of selling some of the others, those which bore the mark of her husband, like the armchair Roland used to sit in to read his newspaper. Tonight, she wanted to feel at home here. The last time she had met Samy, she had felt a ludicrous sense of shame, as though she were an adulteress walking out on the marital home. Juliette had never cheated on Roland, except on two occasions which in her eyes didn't count. She had had a bit to drink. It was a long time ago. Tonight she was playing the hostess.

Samy arrived at bang on eight o'clock. He was carrying a bunch of red roses. He had come prepared. Juliette gave him a tour of the flat before offering him a drink. Both of them emptied their glasses quickly. To the first question Samy asked her, she replied yes.

On the Tuesday before that, Roland had also been shown round a flat, but for another purpose. He was with Kate. As promised, she had taken him along on a viewing, to show him how it was done.

The client who met them at the entrance to a block of luxury flats in Knightsbridge was a businessman from Odessa. A large man dressed in a dark-coloured suit, he spoke little, and when he did, his English was difficult to understand. Roland took against him at first sight. Kate frowned in agreement. The client didn't exactly inspire confidence. As the three of them stepped into the lift, the Ukrainian had given Kate's behind a brief but intense glance, appearing to measure it up for size. He seemed pleased with the goods on offer judging by the smile that momentarily lit up his miserable face.

The apartment was flashy in the extreme. It had been completely remodelled, repainted, decorated and furnished to the taste of the type of clientele likely to acquire a property of this kind. Its seven rooms could have provided the backdrop for a Bollywood film, they were so brightly coloured and twinkling with gold. In the living room, garnet-red drapes fell onto a pink marble floor. And yet the Ukrainian did not appear to be blown away. He went round opening and closing cupboards, tapping the walls, checking the wiring and inbuilt audio equipment, inspecting the windows, guttering and radiators, without asking a single question. The two estate agents – for Kate had introduced Roland as an agent from France keen to set himself up in London – were relegated to bit parts, traipsing silently behind the person apparently now leading the tour.

While their client was absorbed in his investigations, Kate took Roland aside and thanked him for having come. She felt better with him around. The Ukrainian guy gave her the creeps. She had no chance of working her magic on a man like that. When he looked at her, she felt he saw something that could be used once and then thrown away.

'If you weren't here,' she said, 'he'd probably have me pinned to a wall by now.'

Generally speaking, she didn't like working on her own. It was boring when the clients didn't say much, and could sometimes be dangerous, like today. She missed John, on a professional level at least. The Ukrainian had disappeared inside one of the bedrooms. She took the chance to put a deal on the table.

'I'll teach you to sell properties, and in return you'll give me a good fuck, say, once a week.'

Kate was smiling as she spoke. She seemed to have given some serious thought to the terms of the deal she was putting forward, a deal that struck her as win–win.

'Actually, it works more in your favour,' she corrected herself, winking provocatively at Roland. If it wasn't for the Ukrainian, they would have got down to it there and then. But here he was back again already. Roland asked Kate if he could think about it – the work part at least, he teased.

The viewing was coming to an end. The potential buyer wanted to know the exact price of the fixtures and fittings. How much was the sound system worth, and the three TV sets? The drapes hanging across the wide picture window in the living room? And what about the gold curtain rods, were they real gold? Could the estate agent show him the bills to prove it? Kate didn't know what to say. All the furniture, and everything else, she indicated with a sweeping hand gesture that took in the entire living room, was included in the asking price.

'I see,' was all the businessman said in reply, sounding not altogether convinced.

Then without another word, he made himself comfortable on one of the three sofas in the living room and took from his briefcase a laptop, which he immediately turned on. A few moments later, having connected to the internet via an inbuilt dongle, it was clear he had logged on to instant messaging. He closed the laptop with a smile on his lips. He was trying his best to look friendly.

'Very nice apartment,' he conceded. It was spacious, with lots of natural light. He had, however, picked up a number of defects in the pipework. There were not enough radiators. He would have preferred tinted windows on the side facing the road. And so on and so forth. The apartment's downfalls were clear to see; still, it had a certain value, which he judged to be less than thirty per cent of the price the agency were asking. This time Kate really was speechless. She looked over at Roland in despair. He seemed to be finding the situation quite entertaining. The Ukrainian reminded him of a crook he had had locked up about three months before.

Kate fought back more on principle than because she thought it would get her anywhere. She could see this sale was a no-go. The Ukrainian guy had grated on her from the start. If it was up to her, she would have kicked him out of there. But the man wouldn't budge.

'It's way over-priced,' he said with confidence, cutting Kate off mid-sentence.

She was about to call an end to the viewing when Roland stepped in. The vendor, he said, might perhaps be persuaded to knock off fifteen per cent. There was no use trying to get more off, given the quality of the property and its location, he said, pointing out the three sofas and drapes and emphasising with a gesture of his hand the vastness of the living room, which measured no less than eighty square metres; there was no way the price would go any lower.

'*Da*,' replied the businessman. 'We'll think about it,' he said, thereby letting slip that he was working on behalf of a client. Then he put away his laptop and stood up without further comment. He glanced around the living room one last time, appearing to pause for thought, and then he left without saying a word to either agent. Kate and Roland had already ceased to exist as far as he was concerned.

'You're a quick learner,' concluded Kate.

'You see,' said the lieutenant, putting his hands around the boy's waist, 'London is ours.'

Hassan and Roland had their arms wrapped around one another as they leaned against the side of the footbridge running from Embankment to the Southbank. Their eyes gazed off into the night sky. The dome of St Paul's was lit by a full moon. Big Ben suddenly rang its bell, as if to remind them of time passing. It chimed three o'clock. Roland held Hassan tightly in his arms. Their bodies still smelled of sweat in spite of the biting cold that had hit them as they left the Paradise.

'Now what?'

Roland suggested they end the night at his place.

During the cab ride home, sweeping along the deserted streets of central London, Hassan told his story.

'How did you end up in London?' asked Roland, the misgivings he had brushed aside when his body was pressed against the boy's and his head carried away by the beat having returned. He was about to take Hassan home, or rather to John's home, when he knew nothing about the kid, or young man. How old was he anyway?

Roland was beginning to panic when the taxi turned into the road leading up to Victoria station. Sixteen, seventeen at the most. There was still time to stop the cab and leave Hassan where he had found him, on the street. In the dim light of the car, Roland thought he glimpsed a smile of happiness on the young man's face. All at once his worries seemed absurd. A moment later, as the driver stopped at a red, Hassan's face came under the streetlight. There was a wild look in his eyes. The taxi moved off again. They were approaching the station. 'So what if I fall down,' the lieutenant said to himself, before admitting to himself that he had been falling for the boy for some time. The kid put a hand on his thigh. Victoria was rising before them at the corner of the street when Hassan replied.

'I'm nineteen,' he said, turning to look out of the window at the impressive outline of the station. Hassan liked the building because it reminded him of when he first arrived in London. That was a year ago. His flight from Kandahar had landed at Gatwick in the early hours of the morning. He had jumped straight on the Gatwick Express to Victoria. He could still remember how happy he had felt stepping off the train. It was his first sight of Europe. Hassan spoke slowly, his head pinned against the window as though trying to hide the stream of memories rushing up before his eyes. He had fled the Taliban. He had left everything he owned behind. He lived alone in London. Roland tried to picture the things Hassan was talking about. He recalled the news reports on the war in Afghanistan. Hassan had probably seen them too. He could easily be making it all up. The car bombs, the death threats. The lieutenant had no way of verifying Hassan's account. At the police station he wouldn't have let it drop; he would have taken down statements, asked a barrage of questions. He had no desire to do that now.

'Political refugee?' was all he asked.

Hassan turned to answer with a simple nod of the head before snuggling up to Roland's side and kissing him full on the mouth, indifferent to the taxi driver's glances in the rear mirror. A few minutes later the taxi pulled up on Moreton Place outside John's house.

The news had come in that morning. Roland was eating his breakfast after having a lie-in. The previous night had ended at the Cumberland Arms, a pub which had quickly become his local. He had got drunk. He couldn't get his head around the thought of leaving London on Sunday. His investigation had achieved nothing. He was returning to Paris with his tail between his legs, and he would be greeted by nothing but problems when he got there. But did he really have to go? The offer Kate had made on Tuesday seemed a sound one or a surreal one depending on how he looked at it, or rather on how many pints he had drunk. 'I'm not going,' he decided as he stumbled home. The next morning he had woken up feeling fuzzy and heavy-headed. Just like John before him, his first thought was to head to the gym. An hour of exercise would put him back on track. As he sipped his tea, an excellent Earl Grey that John had bought from Harrods, Roland had one ear on Sky News. In Dalston, passers-by had discovered the body of a newborn baby in a bin bag. Manchester United were gearing up to face Fulham the next day. The Prime Minister was in Kabul for twenty-four hours. The succession of stories on a loop was suddenly interrupted to bring a live news item. The port of Dover appeared onscreen.

Early that morning as the cross-Channel ferry approached the coast of England, a passenger had made a grim discovery. A man was found lying in his seat with his eyes rolled back. As soon as the ship came into port, the police had come aboard and no one had been allowed to leave. A murder had been committed. The victim, a man of about forty-five, had been strangled in his sleep. Nothing had been stolen from his person. An hour later a team arrived from Scotland Yard to take over the investigation. There were no credible leads as yet, but it looked like being a major case. A wide shot panned over the area where the ferry had docked, surrounded by a dozen police cars. Then a photograph of the victim appeared onscreen in close-up. Roland almost knocked over his mug; a few minor differences aside, the man could be John Burny's double. He had the same muscular build. His black hair was styled in exactly the same way. Even the nose and prominent cheekbones recalled the Scotsman's features. The resemblance was striking. Only their lips were different. Whereas John's were relatively full, the ferry victim's were extremely thin. But who would have noticed that? The murder had been committed in pitch darkness. Turning this thought process on its head, it was logical to conclude that John may have been mistaken for the man who had just been murdered. John had been killed while the lights were down, and he too had been strangled. The news moved on to another story. A retired couple had just won the EuroMillions. Roland pushed his cup away. He needed a good shower followed by a couple of paracetamol to gather his thoughts.

It was eleven o'clock by the time he made up his mind to call Ranesh. He was surprised not to have heard from him the moment the news broke. The truth was clear for all to see. But the Brit was probably already on his way down to Dover. Roland called his mobile, hanging on the line ring after ring. As usual, Ranesh didn't pick up. Roland tried to leave a message, but the voicemail wasn't working. He tried ringing the switchboard but had no joy there either. The news must have sent them all into a tailspin. They must all be working flat-out, the lieutenant told himself, resolving nevertheless to drop into Ranesh's office after lunch. He was sure to find someone there, even if just a junior officer, to pass on what he had worked out. In a few hours the weekend would start, and Roland had no intention of returning to Paris without shedding some light on this case.

At three o'clock he was in Lewisham in the entrance hall of the concrete building he had first visited less than two weeks earlier. The building had not changed, but for the fact that the Interpol sign had disappeared in favour of the logo of a German import export company. At first Roland rubbed his eyes, wondering if he was dreaming. Then he carefully ran his eyes over the list of all the occupants of the building. There was no mention of any police department. For a moment it occurred to Roland he might have got the wrong building. Yet there were no others like it anywhere near here. In the end he tried Ranesh's mobile again. This time he got an automated voice saying the number had not been recognised.

On his way back into the station to catch a train to Charing Cross, the lieutenant was handed a copy of the *Evening Standard* by an old Jamaican man. The front page was a full-page photograph of the ferry murder victim. The similarity to John Burny was even more obvious on paper. 'Another Case of Counter-Espionage?' ran the headline. A few lines beneath the picture gave a broad overview of the political background, making reference to strained relations between London and Moscow.

On the train, Roland pored over the article dedicated to the case on page three. The journalist appeared to know an awful lot about it. Information must have been leaked. The victim was a Russian agent who had gone over to Her Majesty's Secret Service. His name and age were quoted, along with the circumstances of his decision to switch sides. He was born in Leningrad, as it was then. He had turned forty-five that summer. The details were coming out too quickly for an average police investigation. The British government seemed keen to make a lot of noise about the case. Roland closed the newspaper. He had been taken for a ride. He let his gaze wander over the endless rows of little red-brick houses. As the train entered a tunnel, Desfeuillères caught his reflection in the window. He looked like a puppet whose strings had just been cut.

When he got home, Roland was once again reminded that he was living in John's house. Yet getting to the bottom of who John Burny was no longer mattered much to him. He had lived, and then died an accidental death. He could have lived longer and died another way. Wasn't that true of everyone in the end? Roland was wandering around the flat he would soon have to vacate when he remembered the photos Kate had told him about. They were inside one of the bedroom drawers. Roland thought about it for a minute. What was he going to gain from looking at them? His investigation was over. Did he still have a right to be poking his nose into John's life? He marched into the bedroom with a determined stride. The flat was already on the market. Soon someone would take John's place, and his own, since Roland had gradually slipped his feet into the victim's shoes. The estate agency would draw up an inventory of John's belongings, which would end up being packed off to a charity shop.

At least a hundred photos lay scattered in the bottom of the drawer. Roland gathered them up without looking at them and began ripping them into pieces. Bits of faces, arms and legs fell onto the wooden floor like the pieces of a puzzle that would never be put back together. This time, John was gone for good. Afterwards, Roland fetched a bin bag from the kitchen and swept the last remains of the deceased into it. He thought he was finished with John, but then he caught sight of the laptop he hadn't opened up again since the day he first entered the flat. He turned it on and checked the emails. He scrolled down, scanning quickly over the list of emails. John had received a high number of messages the day after his death. Among them, one name kept coming up: a certain Mohamed. Without thinking, Roland clicked on one of the messages to open it, and was immediately wracked with worry at what skeletons might fall out of the cupboard. Mohamed was writing to John to find out why he hadn't turned up as arranged on Friday 19 September on Place de la Bastille. 'I waited for you until one o'clock in the morning,' said Mohamed. More emails followed. They contained nothing but a barrage of questions. Why wasn't John picking up his phone? Why hadn't he answered any of Mohamed's emails? The initial tone of concern had become more and more insistent until it had eventually turned sour. 'You're nothing but a son of a bitch,' read the final message at the end of the weekend. The first few messages had a photo attached. It had been taken off the subsequent emails. The picture showed young Mohamed in an apprentice butcher's uniform, standing outside his place of work. Roland expanded the picture to take a closer look. At that point, he recognised it as the butcher's on Rue des Pyrénées, where he and Juliette used to get their meat. He had seen Mohamed's face there many times. The young man had stuck in his mind because his wife had often spoken about him. He made her laugh by trying to flirt with her. Roland sat gazing wistfully at the photo for some time; it reminded him of his former life. It had barely been a fortnight since he left Paris, yet the two weeks he had spent in London had changed him more than he could ever have imagined. This photo taken on Rue des Pyrénées took him back to a lost world. By opening these emails, he had indeed let the skeletons out of the cupboard, but they were his skeletons, not John's. Roland studied young Mohamed. John had good taste. The kid was cute. For a second, the lieutenant considered writing back to the young man who seemed to care so much for John, but he soon thought better of it; by now Mohamed had probably found another man on whom to focus his affections. Then Roland pressed the delete button. The messages disappeared one by one.

Back in the living room, he put a CD on to take his mind off things. John had a large collection of pop music, mostly British. The Beatles sat side by side with Pete Doherty. There was almost too much choice. Just then, Roland noticed a CD that had not been taken out of its wrapper. John had stuck a Post-it note on the cover, on which he had written a few words followed by a date: 'Ali – Royal Albert Hall. 12/09/2008.' Intrigued, Roland peeled off the square of yellow paper, revealing to his amazement a copy of Mahler's Tenth Symphony. This further coincidence brought his thoughts back to Juliette once more, but whereas the picture of the butcher's had brought back happy memories, this one was painful. Roland pictured his wife on the sofa with a book in hand, lounging happily in her trademark sprawl while the brass section tutti of the Tenth rang out around the room. He felt a sudden urge to go back in time and change the course of events. He slipped the CD into the player and sat down on the sofa. When the first notes sounded, Roland realised his old life really had come to an end. He looked around the living room. The room felt simultaneously familiar and strange. He wondered if he was dreaming.

Hassan was taking his time in the shower. It was almost four in the morning. Roland could hear him singing a tune in a language he couldn't identify. He thought he recognised snatches of Arabic. The next minute, a surprisingly soft vowel would make him lean more towards Persian, not that he really knew what that sounded like. Turkish, perhaps? What language did they speak in Kandahar? Roland was wondering if it wasn't in fact Kurdish when the sound of running water against the tiles stopped at the same time as the song. A heavy silence returned to the flat. There was no noise from the road, no sign of movement in the rest of the building. Everyone else was asleep at this time of night. The sense of unease that had been niggling Roland on and off all evening had returned to haunt him. He suddenly had a bad feeling about all this. What did he actually know about Hassan? But then the boy in question appeared in the doorway and the lieutenant's doubts melted away at the sight of him. Stark naked, with drops of water still clinging to his skin, the young man wore the same look of unalloyed happiness that Roland thought he had glimpsed on his face shortly before the taxi had dropped them at John's. Roland sat staring at Hassan, dumbstruck, until the boy came up and rubbed against him provocatively. At that point he pulled himself together, suddenly feeling embarrassed.

The living room mirror returned their reflection. He looked old and ridiculous.

'I'm going to have a shower,' he announced to escape the situation.

The sensation of the scorching hot water against his sticky skin calmed him down. He felt himself coming back to life. Scrubbing his body all over with an exfoliating glove, it no longer seemed quite so worn out. He stopped to look at his biceps, which had grown bigger. His stomach seemed to be getting flatter. His legs weren't bad either. With his hair full of shampoo, his thoughts finally turned to what he was going to do next. He had kissed Hassan several times over the course of the night, he had touched him and let himself be touched and it had felt all the more intense for being unfamiliar. But what next? he kept asking himself, though the answer was right in front of him. He spent a long time lathering his hair. But what next? At that moment, he heard the opening notes of Mahler's symphony booming out. Hassan must have turned the volume up to maximum so that Roland could hear it over the water. The sound of someone banging on the ceiling from the floor above reminded Roland what time it was.

'Turn it down!' he shouted across the shower curtain.

The music went off at once. But what next? He just had to go with the flow. When it came down to it, wasn't that exactly what he had been doing all evening? Roland was rinsing his hair with his face tilted towards the shower head when a loud bang made him jump. He turned round. The shower curtain had been pulled across. Hassan was standing facing him in a disturbing pose.

'Shit!' shouted Roland.

Epilogue

Four months later, Roland was coming out of a townhouse on Upper Belgrave Road with Kate. A biting cold snap had descended on London four days earlier. The two friends stood together on the top step of the Victorian house, waiting for the torrential, icy-cold rain to stop pounding the tarmac. Wrapped up warm, they were debating the asking price the vendor had put on the property, the kind of place that didn't come on the market very often, as the owner had repeated several times over the course of the meeting. Roland was of the opinion that the price was unrealistic at a time of economic crisis, but Kate disagreed.

'There's no such thing as a fair price in this city,' she explained to the man who had become her colleague. 'People always want more. I thought you knew that,' she added with a note of irony in her voice.

Roland nodded in agreement. He still had a lot to learn. He was now thinking about the commission he would win if he managed to close the deal on this sale.

No less than thirty thousand pounds, he calculated in his head. And he needed every penny because the mortgage payments on John's flat ate up a significant proportion of his entry-level salary. On top of that, there were Hassan's university fees. Roland had gone overdrawn on his Barclays account the month before.

'You're right,' he said to Kate. 'Fingers crossed. When's the first viewing?'

'Thursday,' she replied. 'It's a Qatari family. I've met the dad. He's thirty-five, nice guy, good-looking. I think he took a shine to me.'

'It's a done deal!' Roland said to himself as he said goodbye to Kate.

It was just past four o'clock but night was already falling over the streets of London. The rain was still battering the pavements. 'Filthy weather!' sighed Roland as he opened his umbrella. Then he turned back to Kate; he had a favour to ask her.

'Will you tell the boss the vendor wouldn't let me go, if he asks where I am?'

'Will you remember my fruit jellies the next time you go back to Paris?'

The reason Roland was in a hurry was because of a text he had received. Hassan was waiting for him at Moreton Place. He had dressed up as a Scotsman – this had become something of a ritual ever since the surprise he had played on Roland the first night he had stayed over. As he finished his shower, Desfeuillères had been scared witless to find Hassan standing in front of him sporting a questionable kilt. The boy was forced to explain that the kilt had been a present from John, brought back from one of his trips to Scotland. Hassan had found it hanging in John's wardrobe while Roland was in the shower and had decided to have a bit of fun.

'I was pissed!' he added, to close the issue.

Since that night, Hassan had taken to sending Roland a brief text to tell him he was wearing the kilt every time he was in the mood for sex.

'Off to join your handsome Scotsman?' Kate asked with a smirk. Since Roland made no attempt to hide the fact, she added, 'You'll grow out of it!'

'You think?' Roland asked doubtfully.

'We grow out of everything in the end!'

They both burst out laughing uncontrollably.